Recipient of a *ForeWord Clarion Five Star Review.* "Outstanding, sophisticated, and mesmerizing…a spiritual intrigue similar to Dan Brown's *The Da Vinci Code*, with the sentimentality of Nicholas Sparks and the realism expected of a hardcore journalist. A gifted storyteller, Williamson pursues her descriptive passages with passion and expresses her emotions with the perceptiveness of a psychologist. Intellectual without being off-putting, this fascinating thriller traverses into an unknown dimension of the human mind—a world peopled with fallen angels and dethroned idols."

"*Bridges* blends vivid imagery from locales as diverse as northern Cameroon to the highlands of Ecuador with one woman's quest for spiritual enlightenment, enduring love, and inner peace. Williamson follows the tribulations of a Peace Corps Volunteer fleeing from her past, but unsure of her future, as she builds and deconstructs relationships with herself, those around her, and – ultimately – a higher power. This is a great book for anyone who has traveled paths both physical and philosophical seeking greater truths and balance in life."

> — Dillon Banerjee, Foreign Service Officer and author of *The Insider's Guide to the Peace Corps: What to Know Before You Go*

"*Bridges* is a winner! This imaginative, exciting, and heartwarming book is sure to inspire a lot of people as it did me. It spoke directly to my soul. Not only that, all the mystery made it such a page-turner. I loved this book."

> — Joshua Tongol, speaker on progressive Christianity, organic church, and author of *So You Thought You Knew*

"Be prepared for an internal shift. In a storyline spanning the world, the author weaves together elements of alchemy, shamanism, numerology, and symbology to unfold a spiritual journey of evolving love that will stir your soul. Something sleeping deep inside will awaken, realize the central truth of this book, and will say, 'Yes, I remember now'."

— Joseph B. Lumpkin, bestselling author of *The Books of Enoch: The Angels, The Watchers and The Nephilim*

"*Bridges* is a thoughtful, literary adventure of mystery and spirituality. Williamson fills her narrative with challenging experiences and beliefs, without seeking to justify any one worldview. The plot drove me to continue down an unexpected path through three different cultures on three different continents. Reminiscent of *The Celestine Prophecy* and *The Alchemist*, these pages left me with satisfying questions about the nature of the world and my place in it."

— Ingrid Anders, author of Earth to Kat Vespucci and Kat Vespucci Takes Taiwan

"*Bridges* tells the story of a young woman's rediscovery and redemption through darkness and light. Pain and disillusionment give rise to a journey through superstitions and fear, questioning and disempowerment—an experience with an ancient and revelatory book of sound vibrations—to renewed understanding and hope in one's ability to create change by following one's heart and being love. Letting go of the past opens the door to living fully in the present."

— The International Alchemy Guild

Bridges

Bridges

an extraordinary
journey of the heart

W. S. Williamson

First published in the United States of America in April 2014 by Agapy LLC, www.agapy.com

Cover design by Zack Williamson.
Cover photo copyright ©2011 123rf.com/profile_petarpaunchev

Interior design by Krister Swartz.

International Standard Book Number: 978-0-9721328-8-6
Library of Congress Control Number: 2013918707

To

my Big Grandma,
Barbara Jean Schaefer,

and

my Little Grandma,
Joy LaJune Williams,

with love.

Acknowledgments

To Fabrizio Guarducci, my dear friend and filmmaker. You believed in me as a thinker and writer, and guided me patiently and consistently with love. There is no way this book could have happened without you.

To other great minds who helped me think through different phases of my writing: Susan J. Bucholtz, Jeremy Z. Williamson, Cynthia Gillard, Diane Nowicki, Valerie Brooks, Janine Felder, and Miranda Ottewell.

To Francisco, Leonardo, and Gabriel, my precious family, for all your patience and love as I spent endless hours writing and rewriting *Bridges* to perfection. I adore you guys!

Last but not least, to God, my strength and hope. You bless me in so many ways, beyond all comprehension. Thank you for the amazing journey writing this book, and all the little bits of wisdom along the way.

1
Into Africa

With the dusk comes the rain, lashing frantically in the wind. Headlights bounce off a stream of water rushing down the street.

Tires screech; a runner dashes across the road and disappears into the bush.

Rain pours and thunder cracks. In the window a middle-aged man is talking to his family. His wife and children are listening; his little girl is crying.

The runner moves through the humid, heavy air, breathing deeply.

Lightning illuminates an obscure room. An older man is on top of a younger woman. His eyes are watching; her eyes are closed.

Water gushes from the runner's shoes as she pounds the ground.

Suddenly the rain and the runner stop. There is a period of silence, darkness . . . and then there is light.

G ood morning, passengers. Please return your seat backs and tray tables to their upright and locked positions; we will be landing shortly."

Jessie opened her eyes, lifted the shade, and squinted out the window. A big, radiant sun was rising over a red-olive landscape. After thirty hours in chaotic airports and cramped planes, they had finally arrived.

A large black woman covered her eyes with one hand and tapped Jessie's shoulder with the other. "Would you mind lowering the shade?" she asked in a thick African accent.

"Oh, sorry," said Jessie, embarrassed. She didn't like to appear oblivious, even though she was at times.

Jessie had long brown hair and brown eyes. Her skin was white and freckled, her body fit and muscular. She was big, with small bones and a youthful, pretty face.

"Where are you from?" the woman asked.

"A small town in Indiana—but I just graduated from the University of Chicago."

The plane landed hard, bouncing. When it finally gripped the runway, the passengers applauded. Jessie turned to look at them—some laughing, some staring out the window, and some still trying to wake up. An old man caught her eye and smiled.

The terminal was a large cement structure that looked more like a garage. As the passengers climbed cautiously down the ladder from the plane, a middle-aged white man dressed in loose-fitting pants and a colorful pullover shirt emerged from the crowd: the director.

"Peace Corps trainees over here," he yelled, waving his hands.

The trainees—of different ages, shapes, and sizes, from all over the United States—stood around, chitchatting. Jessie hung back, watching and listening.

The director was on his phone, running his hand through his hair nervously; the drivers had not yet arrived.

Jessie inhaled deeply. The air smelled dry and sweet. Her eyes wandered across the crowd to a skinny black man sitting on a blanket near the airport wall: a leper, like in the Jesus movies she'd watched. Poor man, she thought. He doesn't have legs.

Jessie walked over to the man and dropped a coin in his cup. He bowed his head and held it there, impassively. When he looked back up, she smiled and nodded.

It was starting to get hot. The director finished his call, put his phone in his pocket, and summoned the trainees to pick up their bags and follow him into the terminal, out of the sun. The terminal was big and empty, without seating or desks, and the air inside smelled of sweat.

After about twenty minutes, the drivers finally arrived. The trainees piled into several four-by-four vehicles, which zoomed away along a dusty dirt road. The windows were open, and wind whipped through, blowing away the smell of sweat. Squinting, Jessie put on her sunglasses.

Africa flew past, the Africa Jessie had imagined: mud-brick houses with thatched roofs, women carrying water on their heads, children running around naked, old men playing cards and drinking from gourds. Wide-eyed, Jessie took everything in.

They reached the center of town, where animals roamed over a massive garbage heap. Jessie, like the other trainees, covered her nose. She had known that Africa was poor, but she hadn't expected such blatant disregard for basic sanitation.

Finally they arrived at a small hotel, two trainees to a room. The carpet was yellow and the walls were covered with painted flowers. There was no air conditioning and the room was hot, and smelled of strong perfume.

After they'd showered and rested for a few hours, they walked to the Peace Corps Center for lunch. A server brought large grape-fruits filled with a creamy fish sauce, fried plantains, and fresh mango juice. Jessie talked a little to the trainees around her, but mostly she listened.

When they'd finished eating, the director stood up.

"Welcome to Cameroon!" His voice carried easily over the hum of conversation. "In this little country you will experience all of Africa: the desert, the rain forest, the mountains, the ocean. And of course lots of food . . ."

He spoke for twenty minutes, and then the trainees filed into a large room to meet their Cameroonian host families. There were more women than men, and many children. Half of the women had their heads covered; some, their faces. A staff member called out names, one at a time. Jessie looked around eagerly when she heard hers. Walking toward her was a beautiful woman with milk-chocolate skin and walnut-colored eyes. Her face was moist and clean, without wrinkles, and she wore a colorful dress, a matching headpiece, and a warm smile.

"Bonjour, ma cherie. Je m'appelle Iya, et je suis ta mère. Bienvenue au Cameroun."

Not yet comfortable speaking French, Jessie smiled and nodded. Then she noticed the prayer mat protruding from Iya's bag and the *mehndi*—henna—decorations on her hands: Iya was Muslim. Starting to panic, Jessie wondered if the Peace Corps would let her switch families if she could find a good reason.

Iya looked Jessie over, as if she were pleased, as Jessie fiddled with the zipper on her bag. After a few moments Iya nudged Jessie to follow some boys, who lifted her bags and carried them to a Peace Corps vehicle.

Five minutes later they pulled up in front of a high wall topped with crushed glass, surrounding a sandy yard. Iya unlocked the strong black iron gate while the driver parked the car.

The boys carried Jessie's bags into a small, simple room outside the house, with walls and floor of unpainted cement. A foam mattress rested on a wooden bed frame, a mosquito net suspended over it. There was a single window secured with bars. Iya closed the door and demonstrated how to lock and unlock it, turning the key several times.

Next, Iya showed Jessie a small washroom inside the house. There was no toilet or shower, just a hole in the cement floor. A towel hung next to a narrow stand filled with toiletries. Iya pointed to a teapot near the hole.

"Tea? In the bathroom?" Jessie asked in broken French.

Iya laughed, then started to demonstrate, pretending to pour water with her right hand and clean with her left. Looking around, Jessie realized that there was no toilet paper anywhere.

They moved to the living area. There were no chairs, but a large Arabian-style rug covered most of the floor, and a hutch against the wall held a display of colorful pots. A little girl was lying on her belly on the rug, writing out the French alphabet. Jessie could smell something cooking.

Iya took off her shoes and sat on the rug next to a stack of plates and two metal bowls with lids. She lifted the lids and began to serve the steaming food. The little girl sat up and came over to eat.

"*Fufu*," said Iya, pointing at a doughy crescent-shaped mound on Jessie's plate with a pool of green sauce next to it. She tore off a small piece, bathed it in the slimy sauce, popped it into her mouth, and licked her fingers clean, her eyebrows like inverted smiles. Jessie removed her shoes, sat down next to Iya on the rug, and did the same.

"Mmm, bon," she said, smiling.

Iya took a deep breath in relief, and put more *fufu* and sauce on Jessie's plate. More silence, more smiling.

When the phone rang, Iya answered, then looked at Jessie and pointed, beaming, at a picture on the wall of a young woman with beautiful eyes. Perhaps she's Iya's daughter, Jessie thought. There were pictures of other young women on the wall, a few young men, and a man who looked older than Iya.

Not wanting to disturb Iya's conversation, Jessie finished eating, then tried to help the little girl with her homework. Instead the little girl helped Jessie, pronouncing each French letter and having Jessie repeat it.

With nighttime approaching, the house seemed cozy. Jessie's belly was full, and she felt peaceful with her new family. I shouldn't have judged them for being Muslim, she thought. They are nice.

After Iya hung up, Jessie pointed at the pictures on the wall with a questioning look.

"They're my family," said Iya.

The house was quiet, and there was no sign of anyone else around. If they were family, where were they? Jessie wondered. With some hesitation, she asked.

"In Yaoundé, with my husband," replied Iya, pointing at his picture.

Jessie considered the distance. Yaoundé, the capital, was twelve hours from Ngaoundéré by train. It seemed that Iya and this little girl lived alone. But who was this little girl, and why wasn't she with the others?

Jessie asked the girl for her name, and she replied, "Regina." Iya told Jessie that Regina was the daughter of one of her sisters, who died after giving birth—a complicated situation.

While Iya was putting Regina to bed, Jessie reflected on her own family. She remembered her mother's tears and her father's unemotional voice when they announced that they were getting a divorce: "We don't love each other anymore, but we will always love you."

It wasn't true, she thought; he never loved us.

When Iya returned, she wrapped her head and covered her body with a long decorative garment. Then she raised the backs of her hands to her shoulders and kneeled toward the east. After touching her palms and forehead to the floor, she rose and repeated this motion several times. Jessie watched with interest; Iya must be serious about her Muslim faith, she thought.

After finishing her prayers, Iya carefully read Jessie's face, as if it were a book.

"Fatigué?" she asked, and pantomimed, resting her head on her hand.

Jessie nodded, and Iya escorted her to the outside room, making sure that she was comfortable and had everything she needed. Saying good night, Iya told Jessie to lock her door and stood outside, waiting until Jessie turned the lock over and it clicked into place, before she returned to the house to close everything up.

After Jessie had locked herself inside, she looked around at her new home. With its cement walls and barred window, the room looked like a prison cell. She took out her sleeping bag and, ducking under the mosquito net, rolled it out on the foam mattress. Then she pulled on her pajamas, brushed her teeth, and settled in.

A huge cockroach was clinging to the wall.

"Okay, Mr. Roach, if you don't bother me, I won't bother you. We leave each other alone. Agreed?"

Jessie turned the lights off and stared into the darkness, thinking about how much she had changed. She had lost herself, but she was starting over. She would find herself again.

The room was hot. Though the window was open, there was no breeze. Jessie unzipped her sleeping bag and kicked it away from her legs. She turned over a few times, trying to get comfortable. Crickets were chirping loudly, but she quickly fell asleep.

Jessie awoke in a cold sweat. Light was streaming through the window; it was morning. She crawled out of her sleeping bag and rummaged through her things until she found her journal, with its flower-print cloth cover and its sweet fragrance. Back in bed, she opened it and wrote:

I had a very strange dream last night. I was sitting in sand, by the sea. The tide brought a deep yearning. Then I saw the yearning: a boy. He came to my lap on a wave. I knew this boy, but I had no memory of how. I loved this boy, but I didn't know where the feeling came from. He was looking down, and I felt his melancholy. He did not belong to this world. I told him that I loved him, and that I was going to help him get home. But he didn't respond. I tried to hold him, but the tide took him away and I wound up only holding myself.

She wanted to write more, the dream had been so intense, but was interrupted by a knock on the door—Iya, who'd come to lead her to the washroom. A large bucket of water, about halfway full, sat on the floor there. Iya added some boiling water from a pot, stirred it around, and put Jessie's hand in to test it. It felt warm; Jessie nodded.

Standing there, barely awake, Jessie was unsure how to proceed. Was she supposed to get in the bucket? Surely it was too small. Or should she just use the water to rinse?

Trying to be helpful, Iya started taking off Jessie's clothes. Jessie was frozen. *Stop!* her mind screamed, but she said nothing, only stood there, stiff as a board.

Iya washed Jessie briskly from head to toe. When she had

finished, and left the room, Jessie wrapped herself in a towel and squatted, hugging her knees, ashamed of her naked body.

After a few deep breaths, Jessie began to cry quietly so Iya could not hear her. *Stop being a baby,* she told herself. *You shouldn't feel humiliated—you should feel humbled. You've just been baptized into a new life.*

After a few more deep breaths, she dried herself off, put on a T-shirt and a pair of jeans, and went out to the living room.

On the rug was a tray with a loaf of French bread, a jar of chocolate spread, and a glass of juice. Jessie sat down next to the tray, again unsure. Should the chocolate be spread on the bread, or the bread dipped in the chocolate, like *fufu?*

Iya looked at Jessie and then sliced the bread open, spread chocolate on it, and handed it to her. Jessie smiled, devouring the entire loaf. It was delicious; she'd never thought of eating bread with chocolate before.

Iya seemed pleased with Jessie's appetite. "Vous êtes grosse et en bonne santé," she said.

Jessie blushed. *Gros* means fat, she knew, and she felt like a pig. Ashamed of herself, how she appeared to others, she vowed to start running again. She had let herself slide, but no more.

After breakfast, Jessie briskly walked to the Peace Corps Center, where she was assigned a straw hut with two other students. Her instructor, a tall, thin, quiet Cameroonian man, passed out a worksheet and indicated that they should fill in the blanks.

Jessie looked it over and sighed. She tried to convince herself that while learning French wasn't going to be easy, she had studied it in college, and she'd successfully accomplished more difficult tasks. For one, she had her black belt in karate.

Jessie's mind drifted back to her sensei and his test: "*Woman, get up!*" He tried to strengthen her spirit for a long time . . . until he took her innocence.

She was still daydreaming when someone abruptly tugged her arm: her French instructor.

"Don't move," he said, his voice level. "There's a king cobra about ten feet to your right. Just stay calm."

Jessie slowly turned her head, her heart racing. The cobra had dark beady eyes, like her sensei. It glared at her and began to slither toward them. A guardsman appeared out of nowhere, jabbing the reptile with a long stick. When it rose up and hissed, he sliced off its head with a machete.

The trainees were awestruck, but for the Africans, this was just everyday reality. Jessie knew this, but she hadn't expected to be confronted with it so quickly. She was thankful for the guardsman's presence, but she was angry inside. *If my father had been there, the serpent would never have invaded my body.*

After a bit of excited chatter, the guardsman took the dangling body to the kitchen, and the class got back to work.

Jessie found it hard to focus, thinking about her sensei. *"Go to the back of the van and get on your hands and knees."* Afterward, he met his wife for lunch, and Jessie went home crying.

Why am I feeling sorry for myself again? she thought. I'm here to move forward, not dwell on the past. Let it go! You told his wife what happened, you left, and it's over. You never have to see him again.

When class was finished, she went back to Iya's house, changed her clothes, and stretched near the gate. She was tired and a bit nauseated, but determined to at least get started with the running she'd promised herself.

As she set off down the dusty road, passersby stared and several women and children began to jog behind her. Jessie felt strange receiving so much attention.

After about a mile or so, Jessie stopped and turned around to walk home. By the time she arrived, her skin was pale and she felt sick. Iya made her hot tea, but she excused herself and went to bed.

In the middle of the night, she awoke with terrible abdominal cramps and impending diarrhea. When she couldn't hold it any longer, she went to find the latrine on the side of the house. A full moon lit the way.

Cautiously Jessie squatted over the hole. There were no privacy walls, but the yard was enclosed. Still, it felt strange. Her heart was beating frantically, and she was anxious to get back to her room.

When she returned, there was a big spider on the wall. She threw a book at it, missing its body and breaking its sac instead. Hundreds of baby spiders scattered everywhere. Burrowing into her sleeping bag, she sobbed herself to sleep.

In the morning Jessie had a fever. She couldn't stop shivering, and wouldn't eat or drink. Iya called a Peace Corps nurse, who moved Jessie to a nearby hotel to monitor the illness more closely. Peace Corps officials didn't use the local hospital; it was considered unsafe. The nurse gave her Tylenol, and she started vomiting. Then a terrible headache set in.

After a full day of misery and testing, they confirmed that she was having a reaction to the typhoid fever vaccination and gave her a cold shower and medicine. Imagining for the first time that she could die like this, she was frightened. Finally the fever went down, but she still felt awful.

Around eight o'clock, she heard a knock at the door. It opened, and Iya peered cautiously into the room and then walked slowly to the edge of the bed. Sitting down, she put one hand on her heart and the other on Jessie's arm, then spoke to the nurse in French.

"Iya wants to know what's wrong with you, what you have. May I tell her?" asked the nurse.

"Yes, please tell her everything . . . also that I really appreciate her coming to visit me."

After the nurse had explained, Iya took Jessie's hand in hers and sat there, without speaking. Jessie felt uncomfortable. When the silence became too much, she pretended to be sleepy. Iya squeezed her hand, bid her good night, and left the room.

"You must be a very special young lady," said the nurse as she took Jessie's temperature.

"What do you mean?"

"A respectable Muslim woman never goes out alone at night, let alone to a hotel. She must really care for you."

Jessie smiled. "I don't know why. I haven't known her for very long, and I haven't done anything to deserve it."

The nurse pulled the sheet up to Jessie's shoulders, making sure that she was well covered.

"Apparently she sees something that she likes in you, or she wouldn't be risking her reputation."

"But she didn't say anything the whole time . . . she just sat there, like she was doing her duty."

"Trust me, she wasn't doing any *duty*. Around here, they believe that silence is the real communication."

"I didn't know that."

The nurse put some medicine and water on the nightstand next to a small toiletry bag and Jessie's journal.

"How are you feeling?"

"Honestly, awful."

"Sorry. I think you'll start feeling better tomorrow. Be sure to take your pills and call if you need help. I'll be back in the morning, *ma cherie*."

"Okay, thanks. Please leave the light on. I'm going to try to read for a while."

The room was silent when the nurse was gone. Jessie opened the drawer of her nightstand, pulling out what she had thought was a Bible. But it wasn't; it was Shakespeare's *Romeo and Juliet*. Struck by the difference between real life and fantasy, she thought to write a new sonnet, and picked up her journal. The words of Elizabeth Barrett Browning crept into her mind and those of Jessie Lynn Freedman took form.

How do they love me?
Let me count the ways.
Birth father, do you love me?
Maybe, but there's a woman I want more.
Sensei, do you love me?
Of course, if you do what I like.
God, do you love me?
Of course, if you obey my commands.
Jesus, do you love me?
Of course, I love everyone.

Jessie, do you love them?

The pen fell from her hand, and she slept.

2
Minding the Gaps

Five arrow-shaped pendants fell to the ground. The witch doctor picked them up and tossed them again, carefully analyzing their position. They all pointed in the same direction, to a spot at the side of the house.

"Allez allez, maintenant!" yelled Iya.

Understanding that Iya was afraid that an evil spirit was going to get her, Jessie moved reluctantly to the house, but once inside, she peered out the window. She watched the witch doctor dig a two-foot hole, reach into it, pull out a small stone, and throw it up like a burning coal.

When it fell to the ground, he began stomping on it and wailing loudly. Jessie thought he looked savage and strange. Then he held up a twig, some green leaves still clinging to it, and danced around for a few minutes before he picked the stone up, screamed fiercely at it, and put it in his pocket.

Iya and the doctor talked in her native tongue a little, and then she paid him and walked into the house. Moving quickly away from the window, Jessie picked up a book and sat on the rug, pretending to read.

Sure enough, Iya came flying into the room, scowling. "I've told you several times now to stay away from loose spirits," she said sternly in French.

Jessie stood up. "Look at me—I'm fine," she said slowly. Her French was much better after a month of intensive language study and immersion.

"You don't know that."

"Because I'm white, do you think I'm weak?"

"No, but spirits can get inside you easier."

"Okay," Jessie said, though she couldn't follow Iya's logic. How could a grown woman believe this stuff? "Do you really feel better now?"

"Yes, not so tired."

"And the spirit making you sick was in that stone?"

"Yes."

"How can you feel better when the spirit was in the stone? It wasn't in you; it was in the stone."

Iya looked frustrated. "I don't know—I'm not a doctor."

"I just don't understand what a spirit in a stone has to do with your not feeling well."

Iya took a deep breath and let it out slowly, then excused herself and went into the kitchen to make dinner. It was obvious that she didn't want to talk, so Jessie continued the conversation with her journal instead.

Living in Africa is like living on another planet. It's completely illogical! People believe that evil spirits hiding outside the body cause illnesses. This means that if a spirit were to get inside my body, as Iya is afraid it could, I would be the source of her sickness. The witch doctor would have to stomp on me and scream at me, like he did with the stone.

When Iya called Jessie for dinner, a stranger was sitting on the rug, a thin man with brown skin and salt-and-pepper hair, dressed in Muslim style with a headpiece.

Wondering if he was Iya's long-lost husband finally showing his face, Jessie nodded and smiled at him.

Iya gave the man and Jessie each a plate of *fufu* and then went across the room and began to eat alone. Why didn't Iya eat with her guest? Jessie wondered. It must have had something to do with male authority.

"Iya tells me you are a good eater," said the man.

Jessie flushed; Iya must have told him that she was fat. It was clear that Iya admired big legs and arms; being muscular and overweight was a mark of strength, beauty. Perhaps it came from food deprivation at some point in history, she thought.

"Yes, I like the food here."

"My name is Samuel, by the way."

"Well, it's nice to finally meet you."

Samuel wrinkled his brow, confused. "Finally meet me?"

"Aren't you Iya's husband?"

He relaxed his brow and chuckled.

"Oh no, I'm just a friend."

Jessie wondered what a friend was doing in the house at night. She knew this was not acceptable in the Cameroonian culture for unmarried persons of the opposite sex.

"Iya has a husband, no?" she asked, already knowing the answer, but curious about what he'd say.

"Yes—he lives in Yaoundé with his other wife."

"Are *you* married?"

"Yes, I am."

"How many wives?"

"Two."

Jessie sat up straight and took a deep breath. If he had two wives, he could explain some things.

"So, I was wondering—and you don't have to answer if you don't want—why do Muslim men take more than one wife?"

He smiled and stretched his legs out in front of him, crossing them at the ankles. Her French instructor had told them that leg crossing is a sign of authority in West African culture.

"Why did *your* father take only *one* wife?" he asked, knowing she could not answer.

Jessie was agitated, but she tried not to show it. "Because he loved her, of course!"

Samuel cleared his throat and leaned forward, narrowing his eyes and tightening his lips. "Loved? As in the past? And it ended?"

Feeling self-conscious, Jessie broke eye contact and hunched her back. It seemed that Iya had told him about her parents, too.

"They're divorced," she said.

"I'm sorry. The Muslim way is more caring."

"How? What do you mean?"

"If a man gets bored, he doesn't throw away his wife, he just takes another. If he dies, his brother takes his wife and children."

"That's very nice, but why do men get married in the first place, if they're just going to get bored and look for more women? It seems kind of pointless."

Samuel chuckled, as if he thought Jessie naive.

"To build a family, of course. It's not easy for one woman to take care of her husband and have many children too. We actually do our wives a favor when we take several."

Jessie bit her lower lip, thinking that this was absurd, but not knowing how to respond. Meanwhile, Samuel caught Iya's eyes with a seductive glance. She was writing with a piece of bamboo carved like a pencil, dipping it into ink and forming symbols on a small wooden board.

"What is she doing?" asked Jessie.

"Writing her prayer to Allah."

Iya washed the board in a bowl and drank the inky water. Then she knelt, closed her eyes, and started chanting softly.

Jessie watched closely, pondering the meaning of *consuming* prayers, taking them into ourselves. It was clear that Iya was a very faithful Muslim. But why? Did she really believe? Or was she praying out of fear for her life?

"Do you pray?" asked Samuel.

"Yes, but not like that."

"To whom do you pray?"

His curiosity seemed genuine, but she wondered why. "To God, of course."

"Yes, but to which one?"

Jessie was confused. Did he mean Allah or Jehovah? Or did he think she had many gods to choose from? "In Christianity, there's only one God, the Father."

"And what about the mother and the son? You don't pray to them, too?"

Jessie tried to see Christianity for a moment from a Muslim perspective. She knew that Muslims have one god; Samuel probably didn't understand the trinity.

"We pray to the father through the son. But it's not a god family, the way it looks. The father and the son are one."

"So you honor the father and the son—but what about the mother?"

"She was human—just a tool, to allow the living god to come to earth and save humankind."

"But the son was also human, no?"

Jessie took a deep breath. "Yes. It's complicated."

Iya stopped chanting, stood up, and spoke to Samuel in another language. "I have to go," said Samuel, telling them both good night. Jessie said good night, too, and went to her room. She plopped down on her bed, wondering why religion was so complicated.

Not long after, hearing a noise outside, Jessie crept out of bed to look out the window. It was Samuel, tiptoeing around the house to the back door. *I knew it!*

"Robbia!" Jessie shouted, sitting up. It took a moment before she realized she'd been having a dream, about a mysterious woman she met in college. Robbia had come into her life for just a few days, when Jessie was struggling. She'd helped Jessie, and then she disappeared.

The sun was out, and Jessie could hear the clanking of pots and pans. A rooster was crowing. She looked at her watch. It was already seven o'clock; she didn't have much time before breakfast.

She fumbled around for her journal in her bag and took it back to bed, where she opened it to the inscription on the inside cover.

My dear Jessie,

This journal is for you to write down your thoughts and feelings. It will help you get to know yourself and discover God, who is Love.

Sursum corda,
Robbia

When life was gritty, this journal had been her one true friend. She knew that without it, she would never have started writing.

After breakfast, Jessie walked to the Peace Corps Center. The trainees were going to visit the Lamido, the traditional Islamic leader.

The Lamido wore a white robe with a turban on his head. One woman was massaging his feet, while another fed him grapes.

Oh boy, Jessie thought, annoyed; a fat man who looked like Jabba the Hutt, with six wives and over twenty concubines. The other trainees took photographs of each other with the Lamido, while Jessie stood back and watched. She didn't want to be there.

A slender middle-aged trainee, one of Jessie's classmates, approached her. Anna had stringy blond hair and thick glasses. Her husband had left her for another woman, and she'd decided to join the Peace Corps.

"It makes me sick, too," she whispered.

Jessie looked at her, puzzled.

"I mean, the way they use women. They're power hungry and oppressive—they act like babies."

"You're right . . . it's disgusting," said Jessie.

"They don't understand the true meaning of *helpmeet* . . . or they don't want to understand."

"Helpmeet? What do you mean?"

"You know, in the book of Genesis. God created woman to be Adam's helpmeet. It's the reason why we're here."

Jessie rolled her eyes. "I'm sorry, but I don't believe that woman was made to be man's assistant."

Anna chuckled, as if Jessie had misunderstood.

"The Hebrew word for this kind of help is *ezer*. In the Bible, it is used to describe God's relationship to man."

"Are you saying that woman is supposed to be a godly help to man, not a personal assistant?"

"Exactly. The Hebrew word for 'meet' is *kenegdo*, which means 'the opposing help.' So a man's helpmeet, literally, is 'godly help in the form of his opposite.' "

Jessie opened her mouth, but before she could speak, Anna continued, "Man needs woman to help him reach God. She plays an important role in his salvation."

"That's what I've always felt in my heart, but the church says differently. Man has his own agenda, ugly and destructive."

"Actually, in the Jewish religion, it is the woman who leads the man to God. In fact, in Orthodox circles, men are required to attend synagogue more often than women because they are considered to be weaker in devotion."

"Really? That's great. I don't know much about Judaism. I come from a Christian background, although I'm not a typical Christian, and I wasn't raised in a church."

"I was raised Jewish, but I'm not a typical Jew either, and I don't really go to synagogue. There are problems with every religion."

When the trainees had finished taking pictures and speaking with the Lamido, the group leader motioned for them to leave, and they all walked back to the center. They ate lunch in the cafeteria, spent a few hours in French class, and then went home.

As she walked through the gate, Jessie saw that Iya was doing laundry, rubbing soap on each piece of clothing before laying it on the cement, where she scrubbed it with a brush. Jessie greeted her, threw her backpack in her room, and went to the washroom. A moment later, she screamed. Iya ran up to find Jessie backed into a corner, pointing at the hole, where a large tarantula crouched on the edge.

Iya took a deep breath of relief, dropped her arms, and rolled her eyes. Smirking, she fetched a broom from the other room, carefully sweeping the critter into a bowl and carrying it outside. It was obvious that she thought Jessie was a wimp.

After a quick run, Jessie went back to her room and lay on the bed. Opening her journal, she stared at it for a long time, thinking about what to write.

There was a knock on the door.

"It's time for dinner," Iya called loudly.

Jessie put away her journal and went to the living room. Iya and Regina were already sitting on the rug, eating *fufu*, and Jessie realized that she was hungry.

"Your laundry is drying outside, Jessie," said Iya. "Be sure to pick it up before you go to bed—it's going to rain tonight. You can put it back out in the morning, or I can."

Jessie nodded, her mouth full of food. "So where did you take the tarantula?"

"I put it outside. Maybe it's here for a reason, though."

"A reason?"

"If it has a message for you, then you'll want to know."

Jessie was tired, and she couldn't follow Iya's logic. Silently she finished her dinner and went to get her laundry. With clothes draped over her arm, she picked up her shoe by the inside heel. Something tickled her finger, and she dropped it. Out crawled a tarantula.

Jessie screamed, and Iya came running outside. "I told you," she said, seeing the spider. "That tarantula has a message."

Jessie was frustrated. She didn't understand Iya, and she didn't like tarantulas. She wasn't as tough as she'd thought, she realized.

"Did you put this in my shoe?" she asked.

"No!" said Iya, offended.

"Near my shoe?"

"No! I put it over there, behind the house."

"Please, just take it away from here!"

Iya scooped the creature back into Jessie's shoe and disappeared, and Jessie, her heart pumping frantically, lay down on the living room rug next to Regina, who was doing her homework. With her hands behind her head, Jessie closed her eyes, thinking about how much she had already experienced in Cameroon. Even when times were tough, she thought, she'd stuck it out. She was proud she'd had the courage to start over, leaving her sensei, her family, and her friends behind.

An hour later the door swung open, waking Jessie. She looked around; Regina had already gone to bed, and she didn't know how long she'd been asleep. Iya was in the doorway, looking terrified.

"Iya. You scared me! What's going on?"

"I took the tarantula to the *ngambe* man."

"*Ngambe* man?"

"The spider diviner. He put the tarantula in an empty nest with grass on top. When it came out—"

"I hope you didn't bring the tarantula back here," Jessie interrupted.

Iya swallowed hard, and tears came to her eyes.

"He said your life is in danger, Jessie."

"What does that mean?"

"He didn't know exactly, but he saw you dead! You had blood all over your face."

There was a strained silence.

"A *ngambe* man who has never met me just told you that I'm going to die? How can he know this? How can you believe it?"

Iya motioned Jessie to sit down on the rug, and stooped to hang a small pendant around Jessie's neck. Then, her face tight with worry, she took out her prayer board.

Jessie watched as Iya dipped her pen into the plant-based ink and wrote something in Arabic, over and over again. Thinking about the fearful world in which Iya lived, Jessie felt bad for her. She could see that Iya believed the spider diviner, that she was very afraid.

"Iya, can you try to explain this?"

"I told you everything. Now I'm praying."

Iya's concern touched Jessie's heart, but she was confused. She didn't know what to think or do. Without words, she lay back down on the rug, trying to make sense of things.

Several hours went by, and Jessie didn't move. Suddenly everything seemed to shift, and she found herself in a strange place. It was all different somehow. Where was she? Why was it so quiet? Was she dead? She wiggled her fingers and toes. *I can move, so I can't be dead. Am I buried . . . alive?*

She slowly opened her eyes, but nothing changed—there was nothing but darkness. She felt for the rug beneath her, with its familiar texture. Then she rolled over on her side and pulled up her knees. A cricket was chirping, very close. She stood up, wincing, her eyes adjusting slowly. She squinted, and a vague impression of the room swam into view.

To her amazement, at the far side of the room, Iya was still praying.

3
The Ancient Book

Two months had gone by since Jessie came to Africa. Bouncing down a dusty road in the back of a pickup truck, she and two other trainees gripped the sides tightly. The wind blowing through their hair smelled of sweet corn and millet.

Some children waved; Jessie waved back, trying to push away a straggly looking chicken with her foot. She gently nudged it away, but it kept coming back, clucking at her. Then it started pecking her shoe.

The truck slowed to creep along two thick planks straddling a ravine. Remembering the tarantula's message, Jessie wondered if this was how she would die. Iya's constant reminders had her on edge, always looking for dangerous situations.

When the back tires reached the other side, Jessie released the breath she'd been holding. Some children were running after the truck, trying to jump on the back. One of them succeeded, but when he realized he was alone, he jumped off again before the truck could pick up speed.

After several hours, the truck arrived at a village in the north of Cameroon. It was dustier than Ngaoundéré; it felt deeper in the desert. The three trainees jumped off the back and ran to the latrine, while the other passengers and the chickens went their own ways.

When they'd all come out of the latrine, a young white woman approached to welcome them. Sara, the volunteer host, was tall and thin, her long hair pulled back in a ponytail. After they introduced themselves, she went over the schedule. Since it was a weekend, they wouldn't be seeing any patients. Instead, they'd paint a mural on the outside wall, with some locals. The trainees were excited to do something creative; most of their training had been technical.

Sara showed them around, taking them past some thatched houses on the outskirts of town and up a rocky hill. The children were dirty, with swollen abdomens and skinny limbs. A few women were bare chested; their breasts looked drained, almost ironed flat.

One of the families gave the trainees some cucumbers, but the Peace Corps nurses had taught them to wash fruits and vegetables with purified water and always peel to avoid getting parasites and other diseases, so they didn't eat them.

"The name of my village, Mémé, means 'the stuff inside that carries culture,' " said Sara.

"That's interesting," said Kate, one of the trainees.

"I wonder where that came from," said Jessie.

"Probably from missionaries," Anna replied. "I'm sure there have been a lot over the centuries."

After the tour they ate a quick lunch at Sara's house and walked to a large open area on the edge of town, flanked by a few houses and several giant piles of cotton. Some children brought peanuts and mango juice. An old woman with a great big toothless smile appeared. Like most Cameroonian women, she was dressed simply in a wraparound skirt, T-shirt, and sandals.

"This is Kianga, our village sage," said Sara. "She's the owner of all this cotton."

Jessie was pleasantly surprised to find a woman in the role of sage and proprietor. Kianga bear-hugged each of the trainees and spoke to the group in her native tongue.

"Today is your lucky day," said Sara, translating. "It's the cotton harvest. Go ahead—climb up on the piles and jump around, or just relax!"

Jessie climbed up a big pile of cotton, raised her arms, and fell backward. As she sank in, she tried to look right and left, but all she could see was dry, rocky mountains and the sky. Exhausted, she drifted off to sleep.

After several hours, Jessie woke to cool nighttime air and the sound of chatter. She pulled herself up to sitting and looked around. Hundreds of people were standing in front of a platform set up on the edge of the area. "Kianga is ready!" shouted a villager, and everyone fell silent. Jessie shifted in the cotton to get more comfortable, prepared to glean some wisdom.

"One day, there was a poor village boy named Baako," Kianga began in her native tongue, Sara translating. "He was sitting in a doctor's office, with diarrhea, when he noticed a missionary girl chewing. She kept chewing and never swallowed.

" 'What are you eating?' asked Baako.

" 'I'm not eating, I'm chewing gum,' replied the girl, with a strange look on her face.

" 'Why do you chew but not eat?'

" 'It's gum! Do you want some?'

"Baako nodded, and the missionary girl gave him a piece of gum. First Baako smelled it. Then he unwrapped the gum and put it in his mouth."

Kianga waved a piece of gum in the air, put it in her mouth, and attempted to chew, smacking up and down with no teeth. Everyone laughed. Then she continued the story.

"Baako chewed for a long time, until his jaw grew very tired. Then he had an idea. He went to the latrine, pulled down his pants, and stuck it in his behind."

Kianga pretended to do the same thing. She took her gum and put it down the inside back of her skirt, wiggling her hips back and forth. The crowd roared with laughter.

Jessie laughed, too, but she was confused. Sages were supposed to share great wisdom, not jokes. Had she misheard, taking another word for *sage*?

The hum of conversation started again. Musicians started playing, and people got up to dance. Jessie took a deep breath of the night air and let herself fall back into the cotton. The sky was full of stars. They had been there all along; she just couldn't see them through the sunlight and clouds.

After a few moments Jessie heard someone approaching through the cotton behind her. Hoping she'd be left alone, she closed her eyes and pretended to be asleep, but she could hear someone shuffling around and lying down next to her. Who would be so bold? she wondered.

"Fair lady, why do you think we are here?" A man was speaking with a French accent. "Please don't open your eyes."

Surely he wouldn't be talking to her if he believed she was asleep. Still, Jessie didn't answer.

"All these people are playing a part . . . on a stage. They're so consumed in their performance that they don't see real people around them."

Yes, and I too am acting, she thought. Did he know? Was he just trying to be clever?

"Only you and I are really connecting," he continued, "communicating with each other."

Her eyes still closed, Jessie grinned. "Do I know you?" she asked.

"I'm the one who understands you and what you seek."

"Do you know me?"

"I know you were looking at the stars . . . looking not for answers but for questions."

Jessie shifted in the cotton.

"Don't open your eyes," he said again. "Do you know why we're here?"

"In this world? Or on this pile of cotton?"

"Me and you . . . here, now."

"Tell me."

"To discover our feelings."

Jessie suspected that he was flirting, but she liked it. His voice was beautiful—deep and seductive. Maybe he was an opera singer.

"I don't know what to say." Now she laughed out loud.

"You can start with your name."

"It's Jessie. Can I open my eyes yet?"

"No. What brings you to Cameroon?"

"I'm a Peace Corps trainee."

"What a coincidence. I've felt more peace in these moments than I've ever felt before."

Jessie's grin grew wider—what a smooth talker! He thought himself clever—and he was. Something was happening to her, but she didn't understand it. "So what brings you to Cameroon?"

"I was attending a summit at the Bahá'í Center of Learning, and now I'm just traveling."

"What's Bahá'í? I've never heard of it," said Jessie.

"It's a religion. They believe in one God—that all humanity is one family, and the time has come to unite."

"Interesting . . . Are you Bahá'í?"

"No, the Bahá'í faith is syncretic—it doesn't try to filter good from bad. I let my heart guide me to the truth."

"Then why were you at the summit?"

"Oh, it was a world peace summit. There were leaders from nine major religions. It wasn't just Bahá'í."

"World peace is good, but I'm more spiritual than religious, and I believe the path is within."

"I agree with you completely. I'm the same way," he said. "Okay, you can open your eyes now."

"Why now?" she asked, eyes still closed.

"Because I wanted you to first like me for who I am, not for the way I look."

Jessie turned her face toward him, slowly opening her eyes. His face was wrinkled and tan. He had sea-green eyes and medium-length messy black hair, appearing to be in his late forties, wearing jeans and a button-down shirt, with sandals.

"And what is your name?" asked Jessie.

"I am Daniel Lumiel, *le Beau*," he said with a laugh.

Jessie smiled and studied his face. Apart from his eyes, he wasn't particularly handsome or *beau*, but she felt a pull toward him. They stared at each other, wondering how they were connecting, each feeling it deep inside.

"Beautiful lady, if only we had more time. I'm going back to France tomorrow for an important Communist convention."

"You're a Communist?" asked Jessie, surprised.

"No . . . they're funding my work."

"What kind of work?"

"Mostly research."

"Research for what?"

"Global transformation. Currently I am studying how matter affects consciousness, how it evolves through time, and how to speed up the process."

"Sounds interesting and important."

Daniel shrugged. "So what are you doing in Mémé?"

44

"I'm with two other trainees. We're observing the life of a volunteer here, getting some idea of what it's like to work in a village. Soon we'll be heading to our own villages."

"How long will you be here?"

"Tomorrow we're painting a mural on the wall of the health center, and the next day we'll go back to Ngaoundéré."

"That's great. Bring some good music."

"You mean bring the right *paint*, no?"

"No, I mean music. Sound creates."

"Sound creates?"

"Well, the vibrations do. If you put sand on a flat metal plate, it will respond to different vibrations—sound waves—by shifting to form geometric patterns. Higher frequencies result in more complex patterns."

"I never heard that before."

"That's not all . . . the sounds of vowels from ancient languages have been found to move sand into the shape of their written symbols."

"That's incredible!"

"This is part of my research, to study visible sound and vibration. It's called cymatics."

"To prove that sound is linked to creation?"

"Not to *prove* it; it's already been proven. My goal is to understand how it all works."

Before Jessie could ask more questions, some people began singing and dancing around the piles of cotton. They made their way to Daniel and Jessie, waving for them to come down and join in.

"Well, it seems like they want us to dance," Daniel said, extending his hand.

Holding hands, they climbed down. Jessie took Daniel's arm and swung him around, and they both moved freely to the rhythm of the African beat. Jessie felt fabulous; it had been a long time since she'd danced like this.

After a swirl, Daniel wrapped his arms around Jessie's waist, and Jessie put her arms around his neck. They locked eyes, and she felt a fluttering in her stomach.

"You have a beautiful smile," said Daniel.

Jessie blushed and smiled wider.

"Kalos kai agathos," he continued.

"What's that?" asked Jessie.

"It's ancient Greek for 'beautiful inside and out.' "

Jessie looked down, abashed.

The song ended, and there was a peculiar silence. Then Kianga let out an ululation—"Ohhewwwwwawawawawawa"—and began the next song. Jessie and Daniel looked at each other and laughed.

"I don't think she's making me any wiser, as a sage, but she makes me happy," said Jessie.

"Well, here's something that will make you wiser. The word *happiness* comes from the ancient Greek *eudaimonia*—*eu*, 'good,' and *daimonia*, 'demon.' "

"Good demon?"

"Yes, when your demon becomes good."

"That's very interesting. How many languages do you speak, anyway?"

"Ancient Hebrew, Greek, Aramaic, Latin, French, of course, English, German, Italian, and a few more."

"Wow! I just speak English and a little French."

The crowd had begun to thin out as, one by one, the villagers headed home. Jessie looked at her watch. "Oh my goodness, I didn't realize it was so late. I have to go. Can we keep in touch?"

They sat down for a moment and exchanged contact information. Then Daniel took Jessie's hand and kissed it.

"I wonder if you would do me a favor," he said, taking out

an old burlap bag. "In this bag is an ancient book. Will you keep it safe for me until I return?"

What's he doing? Jessie thought. Maybe he was trying to give her drugs, like in a movie she'd seen. *Not another con man, please.*

"Why can't you take it with you?" she asked.

"It's valuable. I don't want to risk losing it going through airport security. If they confiscate it, I'll never see it again."

"What's it about? Why is it so important?"

"It's part of my research, and there's only one in the world. Try to understand, but don't share it with anyone."

Daniel kissed her softly and looked deeply into her eyes, brushing her cheek with his hand. At first his face was serious, and then he smiled sweetly. Jessie's stomach fluttered with butterflies.

"Okay . . ." She hoped she wouldn't regret this.

"Thank you, my beautiful lady. Remember, don't tell anyone that you have it. Just keep it safe, please. I know I can trust you."

Jessie was glad that he trusted her—but how could he trust anyone so quickly? It seemed suspicious.

At Sara's house, Jessie went straight to the bathroom and locked the door. Carefully, she slid out a hard leather casing with two metal clasps. Unfastening the clasps, she opened it.

The pages were not parchment but loose metal sheets. They all looked the same, without symbols or words. This isn't a book, she thought. She ran her hand over a page and turned it over. It was hard and cool to the touch, worn smooth. All she could see in it was a dull reflection of her face.

There was a knock at the door.

"Hey, Jessie, we're getting ready for tomorrow," yelled Sara. "We need your advice."

"I'm coming. Be right there." Jessie carefully slid the book back into the bag and walked to the door. "Sorry . . . what are we painting tomorrow?" she asked as she opened it.

"We don't know," said Kate. "It has to be something creative and meaningful, related to health and wellness. We need inspiration."

Jessie pretended to think for a moment, even though she already knew what she would say.

"Music is inspiring."

"That's a great idea," said Anna. "Art has always been inspired by music."

"I have a portable stereo we could bring," said Sara, "and all kinds of music to choose from."

They went to look at Sara's collection, and Jessie picked out the most inspirational music she could find: Beethoven, Mozart, Bach.

The next day they met several locals at the health center. Most of them were women. After some discussion about the design, they decided to paint lots of different people surrounded by light. Jessie started the music and they began.

Slowly, after many hours, the image took form. When they were finished, Jessie noticed that the mural looked European, not African, in style. Since most of the painters were African, she wondered how this could be. Maybe it had something to do with the music they were playing while they painted.

Before falling asleep, Jessie thought about what Daniel had

told her about cymatics. Fascinated by the idea that sound creates, she was anxious to look more at Daniel's book, but she couldn't take it out in front of Anna and Kate, who were sharing her room. Instead, she took out her journal.

Daniel was right. The music that I chose influenced the development of the mural. I am sure that different music would have changed it entirely.

All night she dreamed about the boy who came in with the tide. This time sounds came from his mouth, and words appeared in the sand. It was a message of some kind. Jessie tried to read the words, but the waves washed them away.

In the morning the trainees piled back into the pickup truck and headed home. The driver dropped them off at the Peace Corps Center, and Jessie started walking up to Iya's house. Several children ran by, calling out "Nassara, nassara"—"White, white," in Fulfulde—pointing and giggling. Jessie pictured herself as a white pig in a zoo.

Opening the gate, she looked around. It was quiet, and Iya was nowhere in sight, so she went to her room. After changing her clothes and plopping down on the bed, she took out Daniel's book.

There was a knock on the door, and it opened.

"Welcome back," said Iya. "I hope you had a nice trip. What's that?"

Caught off guard, Jessie didn't know what to say. She couldn't hide the book she was holding. "My friend Daniel lent me a book," she said, hoping that Iya wouldn't ask any more.

Iya sat on the bed and smiled. "You're blushing. Who is this Daniel?"

"Just a man I met," Jessie said, trying to sound indifferent.

Iya put her hand on Jessie's and looked seriously at her, her expression odd. "Come on, you can tell me."

Jessie rolled her eyes. "We just met."

"And?"

"And . . . he is nice."

"What did you feel?"

"I don't know."

"Are you sure you don't know?"

"Yes, I'm sure."

"Well, maybe it's love."

Jessie chuckled and shook her head. "I don't even know him."

"I said maybe, that's all."

Jessie took a deep breath, not sure what to say. Outside, Regina was calling for Iya. Iya squeezed Jessie's hand and walked out the door, grinning from ear to ear.

Jessie took a small mirror from her bag and studied her face. What is she talking about? she thought. I'm not blushing.

She opened Daniel's book on her lap. Specks of embedded mineral dust sparkled on a page. She hadn't noticed them before. Were they patterns, or hidden codes? As she lifted the page to look at it more closely, her pendant necklace swung against it, sounding a clear, sweet note. Jessie sat back, intrigued. What a stunning sound, she thought. It speaks without words.

She pored over the pages intently, but could not identify any particular pattern. Since Daniel studied cymatics, she thought, it made sense that the book's language would be sound. She wanted to know more.

4
Living in Language

Iya wrung water out of a piece of clothing, slapped it on a rock, and then handed it to another woman, who hung it up on the clothesline. They were both behind the house, laughing and talking in Fulfulde, when Jessie came around the corner.

"Bonjour, Iya. Bonjour, madame."

Iya translated, and the other woman nodded and smiled.

Jessie noticed the woman's beautifully embroidered blouse. "Je l'aime," she said, looking it over.

The woman touched her blouse and looked at Iya for translation, since she didn't speak French. Iya hesitated for a moment, gave Jessie a strange look, and explained in Fulfulde what Jessie had said.

Nodding and smiling, the woman took off the blouse. Jessie's mouth fell open. Her exposed breasts hanging down, the woman folded the blouse and offered it to Jessie with both arms.

What is she doing? Jessie thought, panicked. Surely she hadn't asked the woman to give her the blouse! No, she'd only said "je l'aime"—"I like it."

Jessie stood helplessly, looking to Iya for direction. "Take the blouse," said Iya. "It's a gift." When Jessie still didn't move, Iya said it again, her face stern. Finally Jessie accepted the blouse; she felt uncomfortable, but she didn't want to insult the woman or hurt her feelings. As soon as she could, she excused herself and went to her room to change for her daily run.

When her guest had left, Iya went to Jessie's room and sat on the bed, looking like a mother about to teach an important lesson. "Ma cherie," she said, "in the Fulfulde language, there's no difference between the words *like* and *want*. Both are the same. My friend was honored that you *wanted* her blouse."

So it's not what I said, but what she heard, Jessie thought. She would have to speak more carefully. "I didn't mean to take it from her; I was just trying to be nice. Now I feel stupid and sorry."

Iya put her hand on Jessie's shoulder. "Don't worry. These misunderstandings happen, especially to white people." She took a deep breath. "Not long ago, a missionary was telling one of my friends about a place where we go after we die. He was using a translator, but she still could not understand."

"Why not?"

Iya chuckled. "In Fulfulde, there's no future tense."

"Really?"

"Yes, so there can be no place that's only in the future. It would have to be here now."

There was no future tense in the ancient Hebrew language either, Jessie realized. "So where do the Fulani go when they die?"

"The Quran says that man was created in paradise, *janna*," said Iya. "We return from where we came."

"If that's the case, then paradise, the Garden of Eden, and heaven are all the same."

The door opened, and a slim young woman with green eyes and light brown skin, about the same age as Jessie, walked in. Jessie recognized her from the photo on the wall. Iya got up to embrace her, and they started chattering in Fulfulde.

Not wanting to disturb them, Jessie tried to slip out of the room, but the woman stopped her.

"Jessie, I'm Amina, Iya's daughter," she said in French. "I've heard so much about you."

Iya and Amina both started chattering again in Fulfulde, glancing sideways at Jessie. Jessie was embarrassed; she knew what they were talking about.

"Iya was just telling me that the more she looks at you, the more beautiful you become," said Amina. "It's a compliment! Usually, the more you look at people, the uglier they become."

"I thought you were talking about how big I am."

"Yes, but we were just admiring. . . . You are so strong and well built, very muscular." Amina touched Jessie's legs. "I wish I was like you."

Jessie looked at Amina's stick-thin body, wondering why this was beautiful in the Western world. "Actually, I wish I was like you," she said. "That's why I run every day, but I can't seem to lose weight. I guess I like food too much."

They laughed.

"Anyway, I have to go running now," said Jessie. "I'll see you later."

"Oh, can I go?" asked Amina.

"Sure. Now?"

"Okay . . . just let me change my clothes. I'll be right back. Don't go away."

Amina picked up her suitcase outside Jessie's room and disappeared into the house, reappearing in a long skirt and no shoes.

"You're going like that?" asked Jessie, disconcerted.

"Yes, let's go!"

Amina started walking to the gate, but Jessie hesitated.

"No shoes?"

"I don't need them."

"Are you sure? I have an extra pair."

"No, thank you, I have my feet."

It's no wonder Africans think we're weak, Jessie thought. We *are* weak! Not only do we wear shoes, we have different ones for every activity.

They started jogging slowly down the dusty road.

"Don't the rocks hurt your feet?" asked Jessie.

"No, not at all. I'm used to it."

As they passed the mosque, they were both silent.

"So how long are you staying?" asked Jessie, finally.

"Just a few months."

"And your father lives in Yaoundé?"

"I've never met my father."

"But Iya said he lives in Yaoundé?"

"That's not my father—that's Iya's husband. My father was an Italian soldier. I have sisters and brothers all over the area."

The same old story, all over the world, Jessie thought. Still, she was surprised; Iya didn't seem promiscuous, and it certainly didn't fit with her commitment to the Muslim faith to be sleeping around with men. "So what's Iya's husband like?" she asked.

"He's like a father to us."

It was clear to Jessie that Amina had misunderstood, but she didn't try to clarify. She was more curious about the situation than about his character anyway.

"Why does he live in Yaoundé?"

"He works there. He has some other wives that make him happy, so he doesn't need Iya around anyway. She likes it better here—it's her choice." There was a long pause. "My mother has a boyfriend," Amina continued finally, "but she doesn't know that I know, so don't tell her. That's why I think she stays here by herself."

"Samuel, right?"

Amina looked surprised. "How did you know?"

"I met him. We talked one night, and I figured out there was something going on."

"I understand her, but I don't like him much."

"I didn't like him, either."

The road had narrowed, but Jessie hadn't noticed. "Watch out!" yelled Amina.

It was too late, though. Jessie's foot went off the edge, her leg twisted, and she fell off the side of the road.

"Crap! Ouch! I think I sprained my ankle. I can't walk."

Amina put Jessie's arm around her neck and helped her limp back to the house. Jessie was sitting on the living room rug, holding her ankle, when Iya walked in.

"I told you to be careful," she exclaimed. "Your life is in danger! How many times do I have to tell you that?"

Jessie looked at Amina to see if she knew about the tarantula's message or not. Amina nodded.

Iya took Amina's arm, and they quickly walked toward the door.

"We'll be back," said Amina, shrugging as if she didn't know where they were going.

Ten minutes later they returned with a traditional doctor. He took out a small container filled with some greasy stuff and massaged it into Jessie's ankle, squeezing intensely.

"Ooh! Ouch!" screamed Jessie.

"Resist the pain," said the doctor.

"What is that?"

"Boa fat. You know . . . the snake? It will help, trust me."

Trust the fat of the serpent? thought Jessie. Never.

After the doctor left, Jessie went to her room to rest. Her ankle was hot, red, and sore, twice as big as it had been before.

She opened Daniel's book and stared at it. She realized that many weeks had passed, and she was no closer to understanding the message in the sound. She moved the book around and watched the light dance over the pages. Unable to find inspiration, she wrote only one line in her journal:

No symbols. No words. How do I read this book?

In the morning, all the pain and swelling had left Jessie's ankle. She got up cautiously, but even when she put her weight on the leg, it didn't hurt. She walked to the living room, flabbergasted. Regina was getting ready for school. Iya and Amina were having breakfast, and neither one looked surprised.

"I told you that you'd feel better after the doctor took care of you," said Iya. "You never believe me."

"Honestly, I don't know what to say," replied Jessie. "The pain is completely gone!"

"So let's go running again after school today," Amina said, grinning.

Iya gave Amina a reprimanding look. "At least give it a few days, and let it heal well."

With half an hour to spare before she had to go, Jessie opened her journal to write about the experience before she forgot. Under her last entry, there was a sentence that she didn't remember writing:

You don't read the book, you listen.

What's this? she thought. She hadn't written this in her journal. Who had? How could someone have gotten into her room?

Jessie ran through all the possibilities in her mind. Glancing down at her watch, she realized that she was late for school and darted out the door.

When she arrived, her classmates looked at her strangely.

"What's wrong?" she asked. "Why are you looking at me like that?"

"They told us that you'd sprained your ankle, and you wouldn't be in class today. Then you come running in like you just finished a marathon."

Jessie shrugged and smiled. "I did sprain my ankle. But some traditional doctor rubbed boa fat on it yesterday, and today it's better."

Her French instructor nodded and smiled, as if he understood, but her classmates looked at each other, raising their eyebrows.

Someone walked in and started passing out mail. He handed Jessie a letter. "Merci beaucoup," she said, putting it in her folder to read later.

The French lesson continued, and Jessie tried to relax into her chair and listen, but she couldn't stop thinking about the writing in her journal. Could someone have entered her room after she'd fallen asleep? She wasn't a heavy sleeper; surely she would have heard. Maybe it had happened when she was having breakfast with Iya and Amina—but there was nobody else around.

"Jessie, you seem distracted. Is everything okay?" asked the instructor.

"Sorry—I'm just tired."

"Well, try to focus. Soon training will be over, and you'll be at your post working, wishing you knew how to speak better French."

"Okay, I'm focusing," she said, but couldn't get her mind off the writing in the journal. I wonder if Daniel's book had anything to do with it, she thought again.

After lunch, Jessie sat under a tree and took out her letter. Strangely, there was no return address, but it was postmarked in France. She opened it carefully.

My dear Jessie,

Greetings from the land of romance. I hope you are well and keeping my book safe. Remember not to tell anyone that you have it. I will explain everything when I see you. I know it's crazy, but I should also tell you that I felt love between us, and I still feel it.

Daniel

Jessie's eyes filled with tears, and she closed them, trying to convince herself that they were just words.

That night, in the privacy of her room, she opened her journal again and reread the line she hadn't written. When she looked more carefully, she realized that it was the answer to her own question.

How do I read this book?
You don't read the book, you listen.

Exhausted, racking her brain for a logical explanation, she opened Daniel's book and studied it. Then she took some coins from her pocket and tossed them onto a page. The book chimed in harmony—too beautiful to be ordinary. Could the meaning be in the sound? It beckoned her to listen.

Just as she was falling asleep, she heard a cry outside. She dragged herself out of bed and opened the door. An orange-striped cat was standing there, meowing.

"Hi, little guy. What are you doing here? Go home." Jessie closed the door and went back to bed, but now there was a scratching noise as well, and the cat's cries were louder, panicky.

When Jessie opened the door, the cat darted into the room and under the bed. A snake was outside, just a few feet away, rearing up and hissing. Jessie slammed the door closed and locked it, her heart beating frantically.

"Okay, kitty, it's just you and me now. Sorry I didn't understand before. We don't speak the same language."

After a moment the cat came out and jumped up on the bed. It sat in front of the open book and stared at it. Jessie watched, intrigued, as the cat placed one paw on the page, its ears tipped forward intently. It hears something, she thought. It's listening. Suddenly the cat meowed. It paused, then meowed again.

Longing to sleep, Jessie closed the book and tucked it away in her suitcase, and the cat darted back under the bed.

In the morning, Jessie pried open her eyes and sat up. She stretched out her arms and sneezed. The orange cat was sleeping on the suitcase. Why is it so attached to that book? she thought.

After getting dressed, she picked up the cat and held it close, stroking it. She'd started to sneeze again, though, so she took the cat to Iya.

"Do you know this little guy? He was meowing outside my door last night, and I saved him from a snake."

Iya took the cat gently from Jessie's arms.

"No, I've never seen him before. He's cute. Do you want to keep him?"

"I can't—I'm allergic to cats. Too bad he's not a puppy. I'd like one for my new post."

"That's a good idea. A dog can protect you. You need to be very careful, Jessie. Spider diviners are rarely wrong."

Jessie nodded and ran out the door before Iya could get started on yet another lecture about the tarantula.

When Jessie got to class, the instructor was already there, preparing his French lesson. "You're early," he said.

"Yes," she replied.

"I can't believe it's the last week of training. Are you excited about graduation?"

"Yes. By the way, do you know of a good tailor? I want to have a dress made."

"Actually, my nephew is a tailor, and he's very good. His name is Patrick, and his shop is just two blocks from here."

After class, Jessie went to the shop and introduced herself. Patrick was a good-looking, muscular man with dreadlocks and light brown skin. He showed her a number of bolts of cloth. After going over all the options, Jessie chose a shiny white fabric with an intricate design.

"Oh, yes," he said. "This one is very beautiful. It will make you look like an angel."

Patrick wrapped a tape measure around Jessie's hips, waist, and chest. She felt that he was attracted to her, but she was not interested. "So when will it be ready?" she asked, avoiding his eyes.

"By the end of the week."

"Great, just in time for graduation. Thank you."

Jessie went home and changed. It was too late to run. She kept thinking about the message in her journal. At dinner, she asked, "Iya, Amina—did either of you write in my journal?"

They looked at each other, puzzled.

"Write what?" asked Amina.

It was obvious that they had no clue what she was talking about.

"Oh, never mind. Maybe I did it myself, without realizing. I was half asleep while I was writing."

On Friday, Jessie returned to the tailor and tried on the dress. Look at those curves, she thought. I've never felt so feminine.

Patrick looked at her admiringly when she came out of the dressing room. "Just as I thought, you look like an angel. Let me just make the waist a little more snug. Have you lost weight?"

Jessie laughed. "I'm trying."

"Well, please don't lose any more."

"Thank you, Patrick. How much do I owe you?"

"Nothing."

"No, how much? I insist," she said firmly.

"Okay, if you insist. The cost is a seat next to you at your Peace Corps graduation. Will that work?"

Jessie chuckled. "Okay, see you tomorrow."

She changed back into her regular clothes, put on her headphones, and walked home. Listening to the music on her iPod, she felt different. As she watched people moving in and out of a rhythm that they could not hear, she wondered about the rhythm of the universe. Is the same thing happening there? she thought. Do we create the rhythm we move to, or does the rhythm move us? She didn't know.

By the time Jessie got home, she felt dazed. She slapped

herself on the face to make sure she was awake. Then she took out her journal and opened it to the page where the answer to her question had appeared. Under it she wrote,

How do I listen?

She closed the journal. She would wait until after graduation to open it again.

5
The Village

The new volunteers stood on the stage, beaming. Cameras clicked and flashed. Finally all the photographs had been taken, and the new graduates dispersed to their tables.

Jessie sat sipping a bottle of beer. The room was crowded, people moving all around her. Suddenly a voice came from behind her.

"Congratulations, Jessie! You made it. You're officially a Peace Corps volunteer."

Jessie turned around. It was Patrick. He sat down next to her, and the waiter brought him a beer.

"Well, thank you. Finally training is over."

"You look gorgeous," he said.

"Thanks again for the dress—it's perfect."

Jessie introduced Patrick to Iya, Amina, and the other volunteers sitting around the table. Her friend Anna walked over and sat down, too.

"Anna, this is Patrick, the man who made my dress."

"Oh, I was just telling Jessie how much I like her dress, and she said you might be coming. Will you make me one like hers?"

Patrick chuckled. "Sure—I just need to get your measurements. You could come by sometime tomorrow."

"Oh, thank you!"

Jessie, noticing the way that Anna was looking at Patrick, hoped that he liked her too.

"So where's your post, Jessie?" asked Anna.

"In Songkolong, a small village between the Adamawa and Northwest Regions."

"That's an interesting area, between the mountains and the desert. Do they speak French or English there?"

"Both, since it's right on the border. How about you? Where are you going to be living?"

"In the bug-infested jungle of the south," replied Anna, jokingly.

"Me, too," said another volunteer.

"I'm in the northwest," said a third.

"Lucky you! The northwest is a nice area," said Jessie.

The volunteers chatted animatedly, making the Africans at the table seem reserved and quiet. After dinner, Patrick asked Jessie for her address; he would write, he said. She thanked him again for the dress, and gave him a hug.

The next morning Jessie loaded the majority of her bags into a Peace Corps vehicle, to be delivered the following week. When she'd finished, she went to the living room to say her good-byes, with mixed emotions. She was sitting on the rug, talking with Amina and Regina, when Iya came in with a gift. Jessie was touched; she hadn't been expecting anything. Strangely, the box was moving.

Jessie unwrapped the gift. There was a yelp, the lid popped off, and a black puppy with pointed ears and brown patches stuck out its head.

"Oh, he's so cute! Thank you."

Iya was trying not to cry, but not succeeding. Amina didn't even try. Jessie picked up the puppy under its two front legs and lifted it in the air. "Ah, it's a boy. I think I'll name him after my sisters. His name will be Rami, for Regina and Amina."

Iya beamed. "Oh, that's nice."

"I am going to miss you so much," said Jessie. "Will you come to visit me sometime? Can I visit you?"

Iya nodded and patted her eyes with a tissue.

"Of course!" said Amina. "I'm going back to Yaoundé in a few weeks, though, so you'll have to visit me there."

"Yaoundé is a big city, and dangerous," said Iya. "Don't forget for one second that your life is in danger."

Jessie nodded. She understood, better than before.

After a few moments Iya handed Jessie a large decorative cloth. Thanking her, Jessie began to fold it up to put into her backpack, but Iya stopped her.

"No, it's for the puppy," she said. She wrapped Rami in the cloth and tied him to Jessie's body, in the front. "You can carry him without arms."

She showed Jessie how to take the carrier off by pulling on the tie, and then how to put it back on. The puppy was jumpy and full of life, but Amina gave him some water infused with herbs to drink. "This will calm him down," she said. "He should sleep most of the way."

Finally the taxi arrived. Jessie hugged them all and looked around nostalgically, thinking about all the experiences she'd had here. Her time in this house was over; she was sad, but excited about what was to come. She climbed in, the puppy slung in front of her and a backpack on her arm, waving good-bye as they started down the hill.

Leaning back in the seat, she took a deep breath. Rami was calming down, getting sleepy nestled against her. "Well, Rami, it's just me and you now. It's going to be a long journey, but at least we have each other."

After Jessie boarded, the train sat in the station for a long time. The passengers settled in, looking for ways to get comfortable in the cramped seats. A few seemed determined to stay awake, constantly eyeing their bags. One woman chewed on a grilled chicken foot, spitting out the tiny toe bones.

It was almost dark when the train finally pulled out, and Rami was sound sleep. Jessie caressed his ears and apprehensively took out her journal. Now, the moment of truth, she thought.

She turned to the page with her last question: "How do I listen?" Underneath it was a new line:

With your heart.

Terrified, Jessie shoved the journal deep into her backpack, stuffing clothing on top of it. What's going on here? she thought. She knew she wasn't crazy . . . it must have been the ancient book that was doing this. For the moment, she wanted to forget.

In the seat in front of Jessie, two men wearing traditional white Islamic clothing, like many men in Cameroon, were talking. Hoping to distract herself, Jessie eavesdropped.

"It was taken," said the first man.

"Argh, how did this happen?"

"After the world peace summit in Buea."

"Do they have any leads?"

"It had to be someone who was at the summit."

"The imam was there, and many other important leaders. Do you think it could have been one of them?"

That was the summit Daniel went to, Jessie realized with a jolt. The sun had just set. Shivering, she held her puppy close. Lowering him to the floor at her feet, she felt inside her backpack to make sure the ancient book was there, under her clothes. She zipped it up tightly and dozed off. She slept uneasily, waking up frequently. The glare of the lights bothered her eyes, so she put on a pair of sunglasses, resting her head on the back of the seat in front of her. It helped, but not much.

Around midnight, the train stopped for a few minutes. She gazed sleepily out the open window, but it was dark; she couldn't make out anything. Without warning, a hand reached up from outside the window and snatched the sunglasses from her face. It wasn't a big loss, but it shook her. Finally she fell asleep again, not waking until just before the train arrived in Yaoundé.

Outside the station, Jessie looked around for a friendly taxi to take her and Rami to the bus. Men tugged at her arms left and right, trying to get her into their cars. They see a white person and smell money, she thought.

Yanking her arm loose, she walked to the street and flagged down a taxi. A beat-up old yellow cab pulled over. The driver had an honest face, so she jumped in.

"How much to the bus station?"

"Twenty-five hundred francs," said the driver.

"*Ki!*"—"No," in Fulfulde. "I'll give you five hundred."

"A thousand."

The streets were congested and chaotic, and the cabbie drove too fast, nearly hitting a few pedestrians. Jessie found herself holding her breath. Finally they arrived at the bus station. She bought a ticket to Bafoussam, the capital of the West Region of Cameroon, four hours away.

The countryside was beautiful, green and lush, with a moist freshness in the air that felt wonderful to Jessie after the dry heat of the desert. Even the people looked different, less thin, with shinier skin.

At Bafoussam she transferred to a minibus that would take her to Bankim, another three hours. She couldn't believe how far it was to her village. By now she was exhausted. I never want to do this again, she thought.

In Bankim, Jessie found a bush taxi, an old Honda Civic without shocks, for the last leg of her journey. Bush taxis don't leave until they are full, so she waited around for a while before it left, with five people in the back and four in the front. For two hours she straddled the stick shift, hugging Rami—who was, amazingly, still asleep—as the car flew down the dirt road, jolting from rut to rut.

Finally they arrived in Songkolong. She climbed out of the vehicle, stiff and sore, her tailbone bruised. People were sitting around together in front of a bar, as if sitting were an occupation in itself. A sloppy-looking man with messy hair, his pants ripped and his shirt untucked, emerged from the bar. Introducing himself as her landlord, he welcomed her to the village. His breath smelled like booze.

The landlord led the way up a narrow path. In about five minutes, they reached the house. It was white, with a wide pink band painted along the bottom of the walls.

He unlocked the door and showed her around. It was one

of the nicest homes in the village, made of cement, not mud brick like the others, and completely furnished, with couches, chairs, a table, and a bed, though there was no rug like at Iya's house. All the rooms had windows, which opened and closed with shutters.

The landlord's wife brought some water and bread, and a container of kerosene for the lamps, and then they gave her the key and left her alone. It was almost dark. Jessie lighted some oil lamps and unpacked her toiletries and pajamas.

She looked around. The place was clean, but primitive. Strange flat spiders seemed to be suction-cupped to the walls; she tried to flick one away, but it wouldn't budge. The house had no electricity, no running water, and no toilet inside, but there was a latrine outside. The kitchen was large, with a simple oven and stove fueled by an attached propane canister. There was no refrigerator.

Outside the house was a small separate bedroom, like the one Jessie had slept in at Iya's house. She prepared it for her puppy and gave him some bread and water. Luckily, he was still sleepy, so he wasn't barking or bouncing off the walls yet.

Jessie filled her belly with bread and warmed some water for a bucket bath. At least she had a washroom with a drain. When she was clean, she brushed her teeth, put sheets on her bed, and sank into the mattress. Utterly exhausted, she passed out in a few minutes.

In the morning Rami woke her, barking excitedly. She opened the door to see seven children outside, playing with him. She tried to communicate with them, but they didn't speak French or English. Still, they came inside.

Jessie asked them where to take the trash, pointing to a bag on the floor. One child jumped up and grabbed it, and the others chased him out the door. A few minutes later they came back with the tampon and toilet roll tubes that she had discarded. Jessie watched in amazement as they made a toy car.

For a long time they played with their car and each other as Jessie unpacked and organized her new home. She gave them some crayons, but they didn't know what to do with them. When she showed them, they were very excited, and made all kinds of drawings.

Late in the morning a man in his midthirties, short and skinny, with a wide boyish face and a smile like the Cheshire cat, appeared in the doorway. "Welcome to Songkolong," he said. "I'm Albert, director of the school. We're so happy to have you here, Jessie. May I show you around and introduce you to the villagers?"

"Thank you. I'm happy to be here."

"Go, go, go," he said, shooing the children away with his hands as if they were a little flock of hens, and they left Jessie's house.

The soil was red, and the hills were lush green. A fresh smell of damp vegetation lingered in the moist air. There were big trees everywhere, monkeys swinging from branch to branch, exactly as Jessie had imagined it.

"Some people here can turn themselves into animals," said Albert. "Did you know that?"

"What do you mean?"

"They just do it temporarily, usually to seek revenge or escape some kind of trouble. Just recently the police were chasing a goat they suspected of being an armed robber, fleeing to Nigeria."

Jessie laughed inside, but she kept a straight face.

They walked around a cornfield with a large wooden post planted in it, a ball of rags tied to the top with grass and leaves.

"What's that?" asked Jessie.

"It's a charm. If a thief tries to steal something from the

field, his belly will swell, and he'll have a terrible case of diarrhea, maybe even fatal."

Jessie raised her eyebrows, thinking of the gum diarrhea
stopper from Kianga's story.

They came back to the center of town, where the taxi had
left Jessie. Here, Albert explained, was where the market was
held every Saturday, where everything happened. There were a
few bars and a tiny store.

Jessie asked Albert if they could stop and pick up a few things.
Taking some hot bread and fruit to the front of the store, Jessie
noticed a headline on the newspaper behind the counter: "Livre
Sacré Volé," Sacred Book Stolen.

"Can I please have a newspaper too?" she asked the clerk,
and stood there holding the paper. Next to the article was a
sketch of the ancient book and a photo of the Bahá'í Center
of Learning, from which it had been stolen. Jessie's heart began
to race. Had Daniel taken the book?

"Is there something wrong, Jessie?" asked Albert.

"No, nothing . . . sorry." She shoved the newspaper into her
shoulder bag with her groceries and took a deep breath, trying
to calm herself.

The door opened, and a woman walked into the store, a baby
strapped to her back.

"Bonjour, Fanta. This is Jessie. She's the new Peace Corps
Volunteer. She'll be working at the health center."

Fanta nodded, whipped the baby off her back, and handed
him to Jessie.

"What do you think of these?" she asked, pointing to the
baby's skin.

With a forced smile, Jessie held the baby stiffly while Fanta
removed its clothes, Albert and the clerk looking on. Worms
were crawling under the baby's skin. Dismayed, Jessie handed
him back, shaking her head.

"I'm sorry, you need to take him to the health center so we can test him," she said, glancing nervously at her own arms to see if any of the worms had jumped onto her. She thought again of the tarantula's omen. Was this how she would die?

They left the store and walked past the school. A group of boys playing soccer in the field waved hello, and Jessie waved back, still thinking about Daniel, the origin of the ancient book, and the tarantula's omen.

While most of the houses were mud brick, some were made from thatch. The houses were widely spaced, which made sense for a population of one thousand. Men were sitting at tables, drinking palm wine, playing cards, and talking. Women cooked and cleaned, babies on their backs.

They came upon a short, bald coal-black man sitting outside, smoking a cigarette. His skin looked like leather dried by the sun.

"This man is responsible for lifting the souls of the dead," said Albert. "He's a juju."

Jessie nodded and smiled. The man spoke in another language, and Albert spoke back.

"I told him you were the new health volunteer," he said to Jessie. "He said you're very welcome here, and he hopes that you can create less work for him."

Jessie laughed. "I hope so too."

They said good-bye and started walking away.

"At certain times of the year, it's dangerous for a woman to be seen by a juju," said Albert. "If he sees her, she can become infertile, or her children may die."

Why do the people here fill their world with so much superstition? Jessie wondered. They seemed consumed by fear.

After visiting several more people, Albert and Jessie meandered to the top of the hill, where three small mud-brick houses sat apart from the rest of the village. Seeing them coming, a child ran into one of the houses, and a man appeared. He motioned for them to sit down, while the child offered them peanuts.

"These families are Bahá'í," said Albert.

"Really?" replied Jessie, then said to the man, "I'm sorry about the loss of your sacred book."

The man looked confused, so Jessie opened her backpack, took out the newspaper, and pointed at the front page. "Maybe you haven't heard."

The man examined the photo and put his hand on his head. "We didn't know about this."

"I'm so sorry—"

"No—I mean, we didn't know there was another book."

"Since it was stolen at the Bahá'í Center, I just assumed it belonged to the Bahá'í," said Jessie.

"We know only one sacred book, the Kitáb-i-Aqdas, the most holy book, written by the Bahá'u'lláh."

The man went into the house and brought out a copy of the sacred book. It looked like any other holy text, words printed on parchment. Jessie glanced through it and then handed it back to him.

"Thank you. It's very interesting."

Strange, she thought. If the book didn't belong to the Bahá'í, then whose book was it? There must a logical explanation.

After their tour of the village, Albert invited Jessie to a meal at his house. His wife was in the kitchen cooking, with a baby on her back, and their three older children were helping to prepare the table.

Albert and Jessie sat down, and Albert's wife greeted them, serving them some chicken and *fufu*. Then she went to the kitchen to eat with the children. Jessie was getting used to this special "white" treatment, but it still bothered her.

After dark, Albert took Jessie home. She was tired, and happy to be alone again. She closed all the windows and doors, secured them tightly, and took the ancient book with her to bed.

"Are you talking through my journal?" she asked the book, as if it were a person. She was still too nervous to open the journal. Then she lay still, listening.

"I can't hear you. You have to speak up."

Eventually, without knowing, she fell asleep.

In the middle of the night something woke her. When she opened her eyes, Daniel was standing in front of her bed. Terrified, she pushed the book off the bed and jumped up. Nobody was there. She looked all around the room and under the bed. Then she checked the front door; it was locked. There was no sign of anyone anywhere.

Help me, God, she thought; I think I'm hallucinating. Maybe it was her malaria prophylaxis.

Jessie got the box of mefloquine and looked over the side effects. Sure enough, the box listed "confusion, extreme fear, vivid dreams, hallucinations, unusual thoughts, anxiety . . ."

She opened her journal. The answers were still there. Desperate, she penned another question:

Who are you?

Finally, she fell asleep.

The next day Jessie started her job. She talked with the doctor, and they decided that she would spend half her time in the local health center. The other half she would spend in communities, doing preventive health education and vaccinations.

The doctor was a light-skinned young Frenchman with a nice smile. He had quit medical school in France and come to Africa, where he could practice without a license. His hair was dark and curly, and his eyes were brown. He lived with his wife behind the health center, in a very nice house.

One morning an older man came to the health center with a puncture wound on the back of his leg. It was the size of a quarter, full of pus, and smelled horrid. There was another wound on the front of his leg, scabbed over. He could barely walk.

"What happened?" asked the doctor.

"This here in front is where I fell. This here in back was made by my brother, to let the spirit out."

"Was the knife clean?"

"I don't know," replied the man. "It was in his pocket."

The doctor examined the wounds. "You have a nasty infection. If you had waited longer, you would surely have lost your leg, but I think we can treat you with a strong antibiotic and lots of rest."

Jessie took the man to the other room and then returned. She put the medical instruments into a pot of boiling water and cleaned up the examining table.

"It must be difficult to be a doctor here," she said.

"Yes, it takes a lot of patience. You should have seen what happened a few months ago. An old man came to see me. I told him that he was dying, and there was nothing I could do. So he went to see a witch doctor, who offered him a way out."

His eyes seemed watery; he wiped them, and forced a smile. Jessie waited for him to regain his composure.

"A few days later, the man started feeling better. His grandson, however, got very sick and died. He was such a beautiful little boy, just five years old. It happened so quickly."

"That's terrible."

"The pastor was very upset and made the man into an example of what a Christian should never do. Black magic is a big problem here."

"Indeed it is . . . people have tried to convince me, but I don't believe in it, honestly."

"Better if you don't believe. Belief is a powerful thing," said the doctor. "It's why we have this problem."

"Come on—things don't happen just because people believe in them."

"Yes, they do. Energy comes from believers, and it shapes the reality in which they live."

"But belief can't take sickness from one person and give it to another. That's impossible."

"It's impossible in your world and mine, because we don't believe that something like that could happen."

The doctor went to the other room to check on his patient. If belief becomes reality, then reality must live in the brain, Jessie thought.

"So what part of the brain is responsible for beliefs?" she asked when he returned. "How do they get there?"

"The whole brain is an engine of beliefs. It takes sensory data, looks for patterns, and infuses them with meaning. Neurons that fire together, wire together; and this creates our world."

"So the only way to change the reality of this place is to change people's beliefs, by rewiring their brains?"

"You got it, Jessie. Something big would have to happen to change the way they see the world."

Jessie looked at her watch. "I have to go. My puppy is waiting for lunch."

He smiled. "My wife is waiting too."

On the way home, Jessie picked up some rice and beans to prepare for lunch. Rami barked incessantly and jumped around, wagging his tail frenetically, until she served him and sat down.

"Mmmmm," she said. "This is good!"

Rami barked once, as if he agreed, and ate until he'd licked the bowl clean. Then he rolled over, and Jessie rubbed his belly with her foot. His mouth was open, tongue hanging out.

A nice breeze was whipping through the windows. Jessie went to get her journal. Under her question, "Who are you?" she found yet another answer:

The Word.

"This is really happening," she said to Rami, "and I never believed it could. I never even imagined it."

Reality is more than belief.

She paced back and forth, not sure what to do. Then she sat back down to write.

In the beginning was the Word, the Word was with God and the Word was God. Are you this Word?

She closed her eyes and opened them again. Below her question on the page, there was a reply:

Yes.

It was all too much. The room spun out of focus, and everything went black.

6
Something Dark

Sunlight seeped in through the cracks in the shutters. Someone was pounding on the door. Jessie opened her eyes. Oh no, I'm late! she thought.

She threw off the sheets, threw on some clothes, and swung open the door.

"I'm so sorry, Doctor. I overslept."

"Don't worry," he said with a chuckle, "we have all day. Time means nothing here."

Jessie brushed her teeth and threw a few things in her backpack, and they started down a footpath to the dirt road. Someone ran up behind them. It was Albert.

"Bonjour," he said. "Are you two going to Atta?"

"We are passing through—going to the small Fulani village up the mountain, on the border," replied the doctor.

"I've never been there," Albert said. "Would you mind if I come?"

The doctor glanced at Jessie, who was gazing at the hills, lost in her own thoughts. "That would be fine."

"So what are you going to do there?"

"Well, the plan is to vaccinate and see if there's anything else the villagers need."

Abruptly Albert turned his attention to Jessie. "I was wondering if you needed any French lessons, Jessie. I'd be happy to help."

"I think I'm doing okay with my French, but thanks for asking," she replied cordially.

After almost three hours of walking, they came over the top of a hill into the remote village. Jessie's feet hurt, and she just wanted to sit down and rest, but as soon as he saw them, a man ran over with a desperate look on his face. "Come, come—hurry!" he said.

They ran after the man to a small house where a woman was lying on her back, naked, very pregnant, and screaming hysterically. Family and friends were pacing back and forth, crying.

"Jessie, can you get some water? She's dehydrated," said the doctor nervously, feeling around her abdomen and inserting his hand into her vagina. "The baby is not descending correctly."

Jessie's heart was racing. The situation didn't look good. She reached into her backpack, pulled out a bottle of water, and poured it into the woman's mouth. The woman kept screaming.

"What's going on?" Jessie whispered to the doctor. But he didn't reply; the color had drained from his face.

Instinctively Jessie slid her hand inside her backpack and laid it on the ancient book, which she carried with her for luck. As she prayed silently, the woman defecated, and a bloody baby's head appeared in the birth canal.

"Thank God!" said the doctor. He pulled the infant free, only to find another head descending the canal. In a matter of minutes the twin babies were crying in symphony, squinting in the light, and the family was laughing joyously, jumping up and down. They thanked the doctor profusely while he continued to check the mother.

"I don't know what happened," said the doctor. "I was sure the baby was turned the other way. It's a miracle. I didn't think she was going to make it."

Jessie wondered if it was the Word from the book. Everything had changed when she touched it.

After the delivery and vaccination clinic, the chief of the village invited the three visitors to have peanuts and corn beer. People crowded around listening to Albert, who was telling stories.

One story was about a man who had charmed a woman to fall in love with him when he suddenly died. Because the woman couldn't find him, she died too. Another was about a man who punched someone. His arm swelled up like a balloon, and the only remedy was to drink urine. Jessie watched the villagers' faces as they listened intently, intrigued.

By the time they got back to Songkolong, it was almost dark. After a bucket bath and some dinner, Jessie went to bed and fell asleep at once.

The next morning, she dragged herself out of bed, her feet very sore, and went to the health center, where there was supposed to be a meeting. Nobody showed up, so she decided to visit the doctor and his wife.

As they sat talking, the doctor's pet monkey climbed on Jessie's shoulders and pulled her hair. Wondering if all monkeys smelled this bad, she tried to cover her nose without being obvious, and gently pushed the monkey away. It wouldn't budge, and the doctor and his wife seemed oblivious, so she gave up. But when the monkey peed on her leg, she'd had enough. She washed the urine off in the bathroom and left.

On the way home, she stopped to see her friend Sonia, who was with some women, making big batches of corn beer and palm wine as they gossiped about other women in the village.

"I thought you had a meeting," said Sonia.

"Nobody showed up," replied Jessie.

"I don't think the villagers like the doctor and his wife. That's probably why," said one of the women.

"Well, what do they expect? Their dogs eat better than our children," added another woman.

"They're too rich," said Sonia. "Have you seen their house, maids, and that big car they drive?"

Jessie didn't think the doctor and his wife were bad people; they just didn't walk in African shoes. In any case, she wasn't comfortable talking about them.

"All I can say is, I can't stand that monkey," she said.

The women burst out laughing.

"Monkeys don't make good pets," said Sonia, smirking.

One of the women gave Jessie some dried fish, *baton de manioc*, and a cup of palm wine. Jessie ate it all with delight. Then she stayed for a while and helped the women with their children while they continued working.

That evening her stomach started to hurt. Around three o'clock in the morning, she woke up shivering with a high fever, diarrhea, and vomiting. Her puppy was barking incessantly from his room outside.

"Stop barking, please!" she yelled.

Rami continued barking, and Jessie put a pillow over her head. This went on for a long five minutes. Suddenly there was a yelp, then silence.

Worried, Jessie crawled from her bed and stood up. Slowly

she made her way to the living room, turned on the porch light, and opened the shutters. A dirty yellow dog with pointed ears was staring at her. Its head was low, and beneath lay her puppy's motionless body.

"Rami . . . Rami . . . Rami!" she called, tears streaming down her cheeks. Why hadn't she come before? I should have listened, she thought, frightened and desperate.

The dog stared at Jessie and moved away slowly, disappearing into the night. She wondered if she should go out now, but she was afraid the dog might come back, or that someone could be lurking outside. Tears streaming down her cheeks, she closed the window, fell to her knees, and started sobbing. When she caught her breath, she crawled back to bed and hugged her pillow. Guilty and sad, she couldn't fall asleep.

In the morning Jessie looked out the window, but her puppy's body was gone. When she opened the door, the dog's body fell into the house. She jumped back, her heart beating frantically. She didn't understand how it had relocated from the ground to being propped against the door.

Gripped with fear, she backed up to the couch. As she stood in terror, contemplating what to do, her friend Carlos appeared. He carefully approached the body and knelt down.

"What happened to Rami?"

"Another dog killed him."

He lifted Rami's head and studied the area around his neck.

"I'm sorry—it looks like the dog bit him in the throat. Do you see these two holes?"

"Yes, but why would another dog do that?"

"Perhaps it wasn't another dog," said Carlos.

"I saw it happen. It was another dog."

"No, what I mean is, maybe it was someone who'd turned himself into a dog to kill Rami."

"You think someone from the village turned himself into a dog to kill Rami?"

"It's quite possible. It's true that it would be strange for another dog to come and bite his throat for no reason."

"But why?" asked Jessie.

"Maybe someone was jealous. Or maybe Rami was stealing food from people's houses."

Or maybe it's me they're after, Jessie thought.

Carlos brought a shovel, and some children who came by to visit dug a hole near the house and buried Rami. Jessie couldn't stop crying. Afterward, the children colored pictures of Rami and taped them on the wall.

When everyone had left, Jessie locked herself in the house, going out only to get water from the well and use the latrine. For days she was sick and depressed. She had begun to believe in the tarantula's omen. Conjuring up her sensei's words, and twisting them in the darkness, she tortured herself through her journal.

"My sweetie, come to me."
His eyes are bright red.
"I will protect you."
His mouth takes my lips.
"I've been waiting . . ."
His hand grabs my thigh.
"Remember, you belong to me."
He takes away my innocence
with the words "I love you."

After five days of solitude, there was a knock at the door. Jessie ignored it. It came again, and she ignored it again. When it came a third time, she got up to open it. It was the pastor of the Baptist church.

"There you are," he said. "We didn't know if you were here or away on a trip."

"I'm here. I just haven't gone out for a few days—I'm still not feeling that well after a bad case of dysentery."

"Well, the reason I stopped by was to see if you might be interested in going to the Mayo Darly Bible Conference with us this weekend."

"A Bible conference?" asked Jessie.

"Actually it's a revival, to wake the dead."

Jessie looked confused.

"Not literally!" the pastor said, laughing. "What I mean is, to bring energy back to the church."

"Oh, okay. It would be good for me to get out of the house, if I'm well enough. Can I let you know later?"

"Okay. Hope you feel better. We'll pray for your healing and that you'll be able to join us."

Jessie needed to do something; she couldn't stay locked up in the house forever. So she forced herself to pack a bag, and the next day she got into a car full of happy, singing Christians. In the middle, squished between two large women, she couldn't relax. The journey was three hours, and not once did they stop singing.

It was early evening when they finally arrived. Jessie squeezed out of the car, stretched her limbs, and took a deep breath. The pastor introduced her to the director of the conference and two missionaries. Later they would have dinner together.

Jessie asked the pastor where she would be staying. He didn't know, he said. Many attendees walked two days barefoot over mountains to get there, he explained, and they would be sleeping on the floors of people's homes. Jessie was nervous; she didn't know what to do.

"I can't sleep on the floor. I'm just getting over being sick.

I don't have a sleeping bag or anything," she said. "And I wouldn't feel safe, either."

"Don't worry, we'll try to find something for you."

After asking around, some missionaries gave her a sheet and a cot to sleep on in the privacy of a cement storage area tucked behind their room. There were no windows, and it was steaming hot. Jessie tossed and turned all night. She didn't sleep a wink.

At seven o'clock, she got dressed and went outside. The sun was out, and people were walking around. She ran into Monique, a friend from her village—a chunky dark lady with broad shoulders and big breasts.

"Hi, Jessie," Monique said. "I didn't know you were going to be here. What a surprise."

"I wasn't expecting to see you here either. It looks like it's going to be a hot day. Do you know where I can get some water and maybe something to eat?"

Monique offered Jessie a piece of her mango, and they walked around together to see if they could find a store. They came upon a speaker surrounded by a crowd of people.

"Satan is a liar and a thief, a roaring lion masquerading as an angel of light," said the speaker. "He gave us black magic in exchange for our happiness."

He looked over the crowd and stopped when his eyes fell on Jessie's face. Their eyes met.

"Someone here today has a mighty purpose in God!" he shouted. "You don't know it yet, but Satan is trying to destroy you."

Jessie wondered if he was just looking at her, or talking to her. Uncomfortable, she looked at Monique instead.

"Do you believe in Satan?" she asked.

"Of course. Don't you?"

"I think he's just an excuse for our own evil."

Monique gave Jessie a strange look. "Do you mean to say we're all evil?"

"Not really. We want to be good, but we don't know how to overcome the bad inside."

"Speaking of bad, did you know there's a Church of Satan nearby?"

"No, I didn't," replied Jessie, alarmed. "What are they doing here?"

"They're trying to get people to follow them by passing out copies of *The Satanic Bible*." Monique pulled a small black book from her bag. "Here's the one they gave me. I'm going to burn it."

Jessie took the book and opened it.

"Be careful, Jessie. It's dangerous."

"I just want to see what it's about."

Jessie read the prologue:

Anton LaVey, the Black Pope, began the road to High Priesthood of the Church of Satan while playing the organ in the carnival at age sixteen. "On Saturday night I would see men lusting after half-naked girls dancing at the carnival, and on Sunday morning when I was playing the organ for tent-show evangelists at the other end of the carnival lot, I would see these same men sitting in the pews with their wives and children, asking God to forgive them and purge them of carnal desires. And the next Saturday night they'd be back at the carnival or some other place of indulgence. I knew then that the Christian Church thrives on hypocrisy."

There was a church pamphlet stuffed in the pages.

Satan is our true creator, and true Satanism is the original religion. It's about empowering and elevating humanity, by embracing and celebrating man's carnal nature. We save our own souls by communicating directly with Satan. Beware of Islam and Christianity, which were invented to remove spiritual powers of the mind and soul from the majority. People who are unaware of these powers, or don't believe they exist, can be easily controlled and manipulated by those who know and are skilled in using them.

Jessie looked at the back of the pamphlet. On it was a serpent symbol, ascending what appeared to be a spine to a human brain. Chills ran through Jessie's body, and she handed it back to Monique, who was very focused on the message.

"Please burn it," she whispered. "It's awful."

Monique nodded, watching the speaker.

Jessie excused herself and continued to look for a store where she could buy some water. When she found one, she bought three bottles and wandered around town. There were throngs of people everywhere, and it occurred to her that this was a very important event.

After guzzling down two bottles, Jessie needed a latrine. She found one behind the school. When she came out, a boa constrictor was coiled up about ten feet in front of her. Startled, she jumped back into the latrine. From there she watched the snake unwind and disappear behind a rock. It was the biggest snake she had ever seen.

Assuming the snake had gone into a hole, Jessie darted from the latrine to the other side of the rock. Curious, she approached slowly and looked around. There was no hole, and there was no way the snake could have fit under the rock. Just to be sure, she moved the rock with her foot. Again, nothing.

Shaken, she went to find the pastor of the Baptist church who'd brought her to the conference. Maybe he could help her. He was busy with the missionaries, but they were getting ready to eat lunch, and they invited Jessie to join them. She sat down and introduced herself.

Some others came over, including the man who had been talking about Satan, a sophisticated-looking African man with gray in his hair and medium-brown skin, wearing nice clothes and shoes. People were watching him admiringly.

The speaker sat down next to Jessie, though several seats were open; she wondered why he chose to sit there. After nodding to the people around him, he invited them all to bow their heads in prayer. Afterward, he invited them to eat and passed the first round of food.

"I'm Pastor Benjamin, from Bafoussam," he said, extending his hand to shake.

"Nice to meet you," said Jessie. "I saw you this morning, speaking to the crowd."

"Yes, I remember you."

"That's amazing, considering I was in the back."

The pastor looked her over and grinned.

"There aren't too many white people around here—I think it's understandable."

"That's true," said Jessie, laughing. "I'm hard to miss, aren't I?"

He chuckled, chewing his food. "So what did you think of the message?"

"I don't know. Honestly, I've never believed in Satan, but there are things I don't understand."

"Things? What things?"

Jessie took a deep breath, wondering whether she should tell him about her bizarre experiences. Because he was a pastor, maybe he could offer an outside perspective, shed some light on her situation.

"First, a spider diviner predicted that my life was in danger.

He didn't know how, but he saw me dead. Then a strange dog killed my puppy in the night. The villagers think it was someone who transformed himself into a dog to seek revenge or do me harm. And just before lunch today, I saw a snake completely disappear."

His face grave, the pastor chewed for almost a minute, nodding. Then he put his hand on Jessie's shoulder.

"So I was right," he said. "There was someone in the audience today with a mighty purpose in God. I felt like it could be you, but I wasn't sure, because you're a woman."

"What do you mean, exactly?"

"The spider divination was no joke. It's clear from your experiences. Satan is trying to destroy you, and your life is in danger because of your mighty purpose."

"What purpose?"

"I have no idea. God doesn't reveal these things, but you'll know when it comes to pass."

"I still don't understand," said Jessie. "If God didn't reveal my purpose, then how would Satan know?"

"He doesn't know your purpose; he sees something in your heart. I saw Satan under your heart, trying to burn it out with fire."

"This was a vision you had during your message?"

"Yes. I have the gift of premonition."

Jessie was quiet, thinking. "Okay, so let's say you're right, and Satan is trying to destroy me. What can I do?"

"Submit to God and follow his every word carefully. That's all you can do."

The pastor started talking to the person on his other side, and Jessie finished her meal quietly, mulling over the idea that Satan could be trying to prevent her from accomplishing some secret purpose. Was all this just a terrible nightmare, or was it the reality of her life?

She tapped the pastor on the shoulder.

"Thanks for your help," she said. "I have to do something before the afternoon events, so I'll see you later."

After he shook her hand good-bye and told her he would pray for her, Jessie went back to the storage area where she was staying and took out her journal. Determined to know the answer, she boldly penned her question.

Who is chasing me?

Quickly she closed her journal and headed to the afternoon events. A number of different sessions and group activities were scheduled, and Jessie sampled as much as she could, amazed by the missionaries' vigorous dedication to serving God.

After a few hours, she went back to her room and bravely opened her journal. There, before her eyes, was a new answer:

Something dark.

Breathing deeply and slowly, she tried to stay calm. Without any doubt, something was chasing her, and it was dark. But why wasn't the Word being more specific? She raked through her mind, hunting down the source of the darkness. Could it be the Word itself, using her journal as a tactic? Was God trying to scare her? Was God even good? A good God wouldn't let Satan pursue her. A good God would protect her from evil. Just like her father, God wasn't there.

What do you mean by something dark? If Satan really exists, then he must have come from some evil in you. You created the tree of the knowledge of good and evil that was in the Garden of Eden. Otherwise, how did it get there?

It's no wonder we are so full of confusion and hypocrisy . . . because you are. I don't understand why you created life in the first place. You make us think and feel, learn and work, change and become, only to rot in the dirt. Life is a waste of time and energy. For what?

If there's something in the ancient book, some purpose for my life, then show me! Tell me what you want me to do! Maybe I should go talk to Daniel about this. Is he my soul mate? Is that what I felt when I met him? Stop scaring me and playing these ridiculous games with my mind. I expect more from God.

7
Confusion

Jessie unlocked the door and threw her bag on the floor. She took out her clothes and toiletries and started putting them away. Before she could finish, Albert walked in and sat on the couch. He looked both smug and annoyed.

"Finally you are home. Where have you been?"

"I was at a Bible conference for a few days."

"Your boyfriend is at my house," Albert said, with a hint of irritation. "He's been waiting for you."

"My boyfriend?"

"Yes, your boyfriend. He didn't have the key to your house, and your landlord is gone. I'll send him over."

She couldn't remember if she'd given Daniel the name of her village. When Albert left, she threw on some eyeliner and mascara. In walked a man with a tight shirt and jeans, smiling and holding out his arms.

"Patrick?"

They embraced, but Jessie was utterly confused. How did making me a dress make him my boyfriend? she thought.

"Didn't you get my letter?" he asked.

"No." Jessie looked confused. "When did you write me?"

"It was more than a month ago."

Albert came in behind him, and they all sat down on the couch. Eagerly, Patrick reached into his bag and pulled out another beautiful dress.

"I kept your measurements," he said, smiling, eyes wide. "The purple will make you a queen."

"I have to go," said Albert, rolling his eyes.

Jessie offered Albert some money for his trouble, and he took it ungratefully as he waltzed out the door. Before she could sit down, Patrick started telling her about the hardships he'd been through, coming to Songkolong. His wallet had been stolen, and he had to sleep in a bus station. She tried to listen, but she kept dozing off.

Unexpectedly, Patrick leaned over and kissed Jessie on the lips. She jumped back, perturbed, and he looked embarrassed. Without saying anything, she got up and moved to the other couch. This time she wanted to be clear.

"How long are you staying?" she asked in a pleasant tone, trying not to appear rude.

"I don't know. I need to rest after that long trip."

Jessie felt guilty. Maybe she had inadvertently led him on; next time she would be more careful.

When the day turned to night, they got in the same bed together, since there wasn't another, and there were no extra sheets for the couch. With Patrick there, Jessie didn't feel comfortable writing in her journal. She turned over, with her back to him, and went to sleep.

The next day, when Jessie returned from work, Patrick was washing clothes, cooking, and cleaning. She put her backpack away, thanked him, and told him she was going running. She wanted to go alone, but he asked sweetly if he could come. Feeling guilty, she said yes.

Day after day, Patrick continued to take care of things around the house, and Jessie continued to feel guilty and frustrated. She didn't want to hurt him, but she missed her time alone, and she was growing more restless.

One evening, three weeks after he arrived, Patrick went into town to change the propane tank. He was gone for a long time, and Jessie opened her journal. There were no new answers, and questions filled her mind.

> *What's wrong with me that I don't have feelings for this man? He's beautiful; he cooks and cleans. What's more, he likes me, and maybe he loves me. Still, there's not an ounce of affection in my body. I feel bad having led him on. He came all the way here to see me, and I don't even care. I'm terrible.*

When Patrick returned, Jessie was beside herself. She hadn't finished writing in her journal and felt like the ancient book was calling her to open it.

The next night Patrick tried to make a move on Jessie when they were in bed. At first she allowed it, but then she stopped.

I need to be honest with him, she thought. We can't choose whom we love. It's time for him to go.

"What do you want from me, Patrick?" she asked.

He took her hand. Jessie didn't like his touch, so she pulled away nonchalantly.

"I was going to wait awhile, but if you really want to know, here goes . . . Will you marry me?" he asked shyly. "I love you, and I promise to take care of you."

Jessie swallowed a large lump in her throat. Was he out of his mind?

"Patrick, we've been together for three weeks! You're a good man for any woman, but I'm not in love with you."

"I don't understand. If I'm a good man, you can learn to love me . . . it just takes time. I think we would make a really nice couple, and our children would be beautiful!"

She knew he was a good man and would make a good husband. But she wanted to feel the way she felt with Daniel, and this could never happen with Patrick.

He doesn't get it, she thought. I have to stop this now.

"I'm in love with someone else," she said.

"But—"

"He lives in France."

"But why didn't you tell me before?"

"I didn't know your intentions and wasn't expecting you to stay this long."

Jessie went to the other room and came back with a wad of money. "I should have paid you for the dress a long time ago. This should cover both. You're a wonderful tailor. Please, go back home and find someone who really loves you."

With tears in his eyes, Patrick went to pack his things. When he came back, he looked into her eyes sadly and hugged her good-bye. She felt terrible, but she knew that she was doing the right thing.

The next day Jessie woke up alone and peaceful. She had her privacy back, and appreciated every minute of it. On the way to work, she walked by some women who were washing their clothes and dishes together in a pond. Didn't they have any common sense?

When she arrived at the health center, there was a man with the doctor. The man looked smug, and the doctor frustrated. "You have to stop infecting others," he said.

As the man left, he brushed Jessie's shoulder and gave her a flirtatious smile.

"What's going on?" she asked.

"He has HIV, and he's still sleeping with women. A pregnant girl was in yesterday, and she told me he is the father. I honestly don't know what to do."

"People are dying not from poverty but from cruelty and ignorance," said Jessie. "All we can do is educate and hope for the best."

"But they don't listen to even the most basic advice. They're more afraid of how their brothers and sisters can curse them than real life-threatening disease."

"I know," said Jessie. "It's frustrating."

Just then a woman walked into the center with a large worm in a jar. "Excuse me, Doctor. This came out of me," she said, handing it to him.

He took her to the examining room while Jessie regained her stomach and prepared for a presentation on safe sex. Three women came, and Jessie demonstrated how to put a condom on a banana. They watched quietly and then practiced with their own bananas.

Afterward, one of the women approached Jessie, eating her banana. She was young, no more than sixteen. Her face was sad and heavy. Jessie motioned her to sit down and smiled warmly.

"Yesterday my friend's husband died," she said. "The village thinks that someone put poison in his cigarette, but I think he had this AIDS you talked about. And I think my friend might be sick too."

"Please tell her to come see us. The doctor can do a blood test to check."

"You probably don't know, but all women who lose their husbands have their head shaved and sleep in the same room with the corpse for three days and nights, without bathing. Even after that, she's not allowed to leave the premises for thirty days."

Jessie was horrified, but she didn't show it.

"Okay, I'll talk to the doctor and see what we can do. Maybe we can go to see her."

After the woman left, Jessie assisted the doctor with more patients and cleaning. Then she told him about the woman whose husband had died. He was sorry, but he didn't want to go to her house.

"Who is going to help?" she asked. "If we don't, nobody will."

"If we go there, people are going to wonder why. It's not a good move culturally or politically. Her husband was a very important man here."

"But—"

"If she has HIV, there's nothing we can do about it anyway. I think you need to forget it, Jessie."

She nodded, but she didn't agree. In her opinion, they had an obligation to help everyone.

The doctor left, and Jessie went home for lunch. As she prepared her food, she remembered Rami and how excited he had been at lunchtime. She missed her puppy and his energy. Life wasn't the same without him.

After lunch and a nap, Jessie opened Daniel's book and stared at the page, listening, looking it over. It had been a while since she looked at it, but now she was ready to find some answers.

"If you created woman as man's spiritual help," she asked the book, "then why do you let man abuse her? I don't understand."

She listened carefully and looked in her journal. Then she threw down a handful of coins on the page.

"No symbols, no patterns, no message, nothing. All you do is chime."

You said you are the Word, the divine language of God. Are you communicating through Daniel's book? I'm sorry I got upset when you told me that something dark was after me. You were just so vague. I want to understand and follow my purpose, whatever it is, but I need more details. Please talk to me again.

When Jessie looked up, she noticed Albert standing in the doorway watching her. She instinctively closed her journal.

"Jessie, you're doing a nice job with the women who go to the health center. They love your presentations."

"Thank you. I'm just glad we all have a chance to get to know each other and become friends."

"The banana bread you taught them how to make was good. I told my wife she should sell it on market day."

"Good idea," said Jessie, feeling a bit nervous.

"Hey, my wife said that you are a black belt in karate. That's really unusual."

"Yes. They thought it was funny that a woman could know karate. I showed them a few things."

"I would never have guessed. Have you ever thought about teaching?"

"I used to teach, but not anymore."

Jessie recalled her black-belt test and what it felt like to be rolling down a hill into a swamp, with her sensei trying to stab her. If she had not blocked, the knife would have hit her throat.

"I'm sure the children would love it," said Albert. "And some adults would come, too."

"Thanks, but I don't really have time."

"At least give it some thought."

Jessie was certain she didn't want to dwell on a martial art that had caused her so much pain, and she politely demurred.

As the weeks passed, Albert and Jessie were becoming good friends, and he started coming over frequently. One day Jessie was sitting on her couch, reading her mail, when he came by with a plastic bag in his hand.

"What do you have?" asked Jessie.

"Today is your lucky day," he said. "I'm going to make you a surprise dinner."

Jessie chuckled and pointed to the kitchen. He pulled his shoulders back and stuck out his chest. Ten minutes later he came out with a big plate of sautéed snake with beans. Jessie ate the beans but left the snake.

"You don't like snake?" he asked.

"No, I'm sorry. But I like the beans. Where did you learn how to cook?"

"My mother couldn't do everything on her own, and she didn't have any girls, so the boys did a lot."

Albert was licking his lips and staring at her like a hungry lion, but Jessie didn't notice. Suddenly he got up.

"You should probably know," he said, "it's hard for me to love a woman. I'm terribly jealous and possessive."

Then he walked out the door. Jessie didn't know what to say or think.

She checked her journal again; there was nothing new. Without inspiration, she went to bed. Her dream was vivid and frightening. Someone pushed her, and she fell for a long time. When her head hit the ground, she awoke.

In the morning, Jessie had a bad headache. She took some Tylenol and went to work. Then she visited her good friend Monique. Her house was modest, and buckets of water and dirty pots were scattered around the yard.

Jessie picked up the baby crawling around in the dust and sat down on a stump. The baby was wet and smelled like urine, so Jessie offered to bathe him while Monique washed the lunch dishes and prepared dinner.

"What are you cooking?" asked Jessie.

"Why don't you guess?" Monique replied.

"Couscous!"

"That's right, with okra and dried fish."

"Hey, I wanted to ask you, did you ever burn that *Satanic Bible*?"

"Yes—why?"

"I just wanted to make sure it was destroyed. It gave me a really bad feeling."

"Me, too. I was so surprised when you told me that you didn't believe in Satan."

"Honestly, I don't know if he's real or not, but either way, I don't want anything to do with him."

"Of course he's real. Otherwise there wouldn't be evil in this world," said Monique.

"You're right. If there's a good God, there must be an evil God, too . . . unless God is both good and evil."

"Satan is not the opposite of God. Satan was created, like you and me."

"I know this. He was Lucifer, the highest angel, created in perfect beauty and wisdom. I just wonder what happened."

"The pastor said he was God's favorite, but he wanted to be worshipped like God. So there was a war, and he was cast down to earth."

"But the Garden of Eden was on earth. Of all the places in the universe, why would he cast a rebellious angel into his garden? Why not a black hole somewhere?"

"I have no idea," replied Monique. "The pastor didn't teach us anything about that."

We cannot cast away a part of ourselves. Jessie smiled, but didn't speak her thoughts. They were both silent for a few moments.

"By the way, what's going on between Albert and you? People are talking."

"What do you mean?" asked Jessie. "Nothing."

"He's been going to see you a lot. People think that maybe you are sleeping with him."

"No! He's married, and he's not my type anyway," said Jessie. "Albert is just a friend, that's all."

"Okay, but be careful. I think he likes you more than as a friend. He's been seeing a witch doctor."

There was a pause.

"For what?" asked Jessie.

"Probably to put a love spell on you."

Here we go again with the black magic. "I'm sorry, but I don't believe in that stuff." Jessie laughed.

"It happens. Why do you think our beautiful women end up with ugly men?"

Jessie chuckled. "People need to worry about themselves."

"Okay, Jessie. I warned you."

"Thank you."

A few days later, Albert asked Jessie to accompany him to a community meeting in Atta. He wanted to create a women's group with all the surrounding villages.

"Why are *you* interested in a women's group?"

"More banana bread," he said, smiling, "and other small business projects. Didn't you teach some women at the health center to make soap, too?"

"Yes," replied Jessie.

"Well, they can make money in the market and help our community."

"Okay, sounds like a good idea. When is it?"

"Tomorrow—Friday."

The next day they walked for more than two hours. The meeting was full of men, and only a few of them were interested in Albert's proposal. With all the items on the agenda, it went much longer than Jessie expected, but there was a nice dinner provided.

By the time dinner was over, Jessie was feeling tired and dizzy. She'd only had one beer, but it felt like many. It was too late to walk home, and she found herself alone with Albert in a small room, with only one bed. Without delay, he attacked her mouth with his and pulled off all her clothing. In a daze, she let him do what he wanted.

When Jessie woke up in the morning, she didn't remember everything that had happened, but she knew that she had slept with him willingly. Albert was on his side, breathing heavily in her ear. The smell of his breath was disgusting.

Confused and disoriented, Jessie climbed over Albert and put on her clothes. Then she cracked open the door. It was late morning, and the sun was shining brightly. People were walking around. Spotting a latrine, she covered her head and strode over.

When she returned, Albert was awake. He grabbed her and threw her down on the bed playfully.

"You are all mine," he said, smiling from ear to ear.

"Albert, I wasn't expecting—"

"I love you!" he said. "Love, love, love you!"

He kissed Jessie, and she couldn't resist him, as if her inner thoughts had been overtaken by an external force.

"But you are married!" she said.

"It was arranged, and it never worked."

"I feel sick. Can we go home now?"

Jessie covered her head as they left Atta. When they were out of the village, on the path back to Songkolong, she took the covering off.

"It's so hot today."

Albert handed her a banana. "Eat this, for energy."

But she was thirsty, not hungry.

"What makes you so sure you love me?" she asked.

"You love me, too, and you know it."

Jessie couldn't remember ever being attracted to Albert, much less falling in love with him. It had come on suddenly, rushed. "Honestly, I don't know what I feel, but maybe it's love. I guess it could be."

"From the way you were moving last night, I think it's clear," he said smugly.

She didn't remember moving, or even enjoying it. Something was terribly wrong.

8
Charmed

A week passed. Every night, Albert stayed at Jessie's house until very late. Every day, Jessie was late to work. She looked so tired and aloof. The villagers were gossiping, and the doctor and his wife were concerned.

Her friend Sonia came to the health center. "Nobody thinks your relationship with Albert is a good thing," she said. "What's going on?"

"Honestly, I don't know. Something happened . . . I haven't been feeling well, and Albert has been taking care of me."

"Albert is a slimeball. He just wants your money and a chance to go to the States."

"He said he loves me."

"Give me a break! He's married with three kids, he can't pay his own rent, and he's looking for a way out."

"That's not what he told me."

"So what did he tell you?"

"When his corn is ready to harvest, he'll have enough money to live well for a year."

"Sure . . . did he tell you that 'his' corn belongs to the schoolchildren? Or that he has borrowed money from several people here and never paid them back?"

Jessie searched her mind for the right words. "Sonia, he's not a bad guy. He wants to start a women's group in our community, and he cares about the schoolchildren, too. He's going to pay people back."

"Bah, I don't think so."

That night Jessie told Albert what the villagers were saying and asked him if it was true. He denied everything, except that he owed some people money. Then he went to his house and came back with a pig.

"Can I put my pig in your latrine?"

"Why?" replied Jessie, confused.

"So we can leave very early to take it to a friend's house. I'm selling it to pay people back."

In the morning Jessie got up and went out to her latrine. Forgetting about the pig, she swung open the door, and it squealed loudly. Alarmed, she slammed the door shut and ran back to the house.

Albert showed up late and told her to pack a bathing suit and some clothes. They were going to be gone all weekend.

After dropping off the pig, they went to the coast, where they stayed at a small hotel patronized mostly by foreigners. For two days they lounged on the beach, swam in the ocean, and dined on fish and eel. Since Albert needed his money to take care of his debts, Jessie paid for everything.

There were no mosquito nets in the hotel, and Jessie returned home with itchy bites all over her body. At work, the doctor gave her some cortisone cream and told her that something had come for her in the mail. Since the houses had no street numbers, everything went to the health center.

Jessie was always excited to get mail, and she opened her letter without delay. It was from Amina, a wedding invitation. Unfortunately, the wedding had already happened; the letter was postmarked over a month before. Jessie thought of her friend fondly and hoped that she was happy with her new husband.

It was a quiet day, with no patients. The doctor left early, and Jessie stayed alone, hoping there wouldn't be any emergencies. To pass the time, she wrote in her journal.

Amina is finally married to Ali. I know that she loves him very much. I'm not sure I feel the same way about Albert. He is kind to take care of me, but others have taken care of me too, and I never felt so docile and empty as now. It's like I'm bound to him through his attraction and affection.

Monique walked through the door.

"So I hear you've been charmed," she said.

"What are you talking about?"

"Albert put a love spell on you, and now you're his woman. I told you to be careful!"

"I don't know what happened. He wanted to create a women's group with the surrounding communities. We went to a meeting in Atta, and everything started there. How would I know if I've been charmed or not?"

"Do you love him?" asked Monique. "Do you feel love in your heart?"

"I feel like he needs me, and I should be there for him. It's not any kind of attraction or connection. Like I told you before, he's not my type."

"How have you felt since you came back from Atta?"

"Not very well. Every morning I wake up nauseated and weak, but Albert has been giving me some herbs that help me feel better."

"I know you don't want to believe it, but you've been charmed! Come with me."

Jessie locked the health center and followed Monique to a witch doctor. With a stone in his hand, he ground up a variety of leaves and grasses into a powder. Then he mixed the powder in a glass of water and told her to drink it. She drank it all, paid him, and walked home. Feeling sleepy, she lay down and took a long nap.

When Albert came over that night, he didn't paw at Jessie's body and take her to bed like usual. Instead, he took her to his landlord's house. Straightaway, he handed the man six thousand CFA francs.

"What's this? You owe me twenty thousand. Pay me now or get your family out of my house," the landlord yelled.

Albert said he didn't have more money, but Jessie knew what he'd received for his pig. It was more than twenty thousand.

They switched languages and started speaking very quickly. Suddenly the landlord turned to Jessie and asked for her identification papers. Albert wrote Jessie's name on what looked like a legal document. Then he pulled her passport from his shoulder bag and handed it to the man.

"Albert, what are you doing? Why do you have my passport? Give it back."

"Don't worry, my love. You're just signing as a witness, and they need your identification papers to proceed."

"What? You never told me anything."

"I'm telling you now. Don't worry!"

Confused and afraid, Jessie grabbed her passport and the shoulder bag and darted out the door. When she got to her house, she opened the bag and found some of her jewelry and the ancient book.

There must be some kind of mistake, she thought. He couldn't possibly have been trying to sell my personal belongings.

She opened the book and watched the light glimmer on the pages. How could she have forgotten? Slipping from her hands, it struck the table and chimed, and she realized that Albert had taken her for a fool.

Just then Albert came running through the door and into the house.

"Get out, Albert!" she shouted. "I never want to see you again."

"What are you talking about?" Albert said calmly. "Let me explain."

"You charmed me, didn't you?"

"No—"

"Yes, you did."

"Okay, I did, but don't worry. Everything is fine."

"No, everything is not fine. Get out!"

Albert moved toward Jessie to give her a hug, but she grabbed the book and held it up like a shield.

"My dear, you belong to me. Put the book down, and let's go to bed."

"The spell has been broken. Go *now!*"

Albert frowned and moved closer. "How did you get that book, anyway?"

Jessie didn't answer.

"How much is it worth?"

"Nothing!" replied Jessie.

There was a long silence, and his eyes narrowed. "That's the book that was stolen," he said. "I found the newspaper article in your drawer."

Jessie tried to stay calm and pretend she didn't know what he was talking about. "No, this book wasn't stolen. It belongs to my friend. He is coming back to get it."

"Okay. Well, then it won't matter if I tell the police about it. You won't be arrested, and they won't confiscate the book."

Afraid, Jessie put the book down and went to bed with him. Every thrust was a jolt of pain and misery.

"Please don't tell anyone about the book," she begged. "Will you promise me?"

"Okay, I promise, but don't leave me. Never leave me. We're going to get married, and I'm going back to the United States with you. Do you understand?"

"Of course," Jessie said, trying to sound affectionate.

Every day Jessie went to work, and every night Albert fed from her body. She was lethargic and numb; it was the only way to get through it. Some way, somehow, she had to escape. The only one she could talk to was her journal, but it was not talking to her anymore.

Albert scares me, and I'm dying inside. I have to find Daniel, but I don't know how. I wrote him weeks ago, and he hasn't responded. Maybe he's upset because I questioned him about the book. I wasn't accusing him of stealing; I just want to know what's going on. Please talk to me—please help me find a way.

Jessie was walking home from work when Albert met her, coming the other way. He looked nervous; something was wrong. He told her that he needed money.

The closest bank was in Bafoussam, a full day away. By the time they got there, it was closed. Jessie withdrew the maximum— one hundred thousand CFA francs, the equivalent of about two hundred dollars—from an ATM, and Albert put it in his pocket. Then he told her that he had to go away for a few weeks.

Since she couldn't make it home before dark, she found a budget hotel. In the morning, she picked up a few supplies, went back to the bank, and withdrew all the rest of her money. In the bathroom, she wrapped it up in a bandanna and tied it around her leg, under her pants.

When she returned to Songkolong, a letter had been pushed under her door. There was no return address, but it was postmarked from France. She tore it open.

My dear Jessie,

I got your letter. Thank you for letting me know about the newspaper article, but I did not steal the book. Please come to me as soon as possible, since I can't come to you now.

Fly into Nice and bring the book. Since the authorities will surely be checking bags at the airport in Cameroon, you must fly out of Nigeria. Call me before you leave.

I will explain everything when you get here. I love you. I've loved you from the moment I saw you lying on the cotton, under the stars. I can't wait to show you how much.

Forever,
Daniel

Her eyes filled with tears.

There was a knock on the door. She opened it to find a man standing outside.

"Ms. Jessie?" he asked, tentatively.

"Yes?"

"Are you okay, ma'am? It looks like you are crying."

"Fine, fine," Jessie replied, wiping her tears. "How can I help you?"

"My name is Nathaniel . . . I'm from Nigeria. I was told to come see you."

"About what?"

"I need to a place to sleep and work, to earn money for my journey home. Long story, but the police detained me. They locked me up and stole all my money."

"The police?"

"They thought I was lying about my national identity, because I have a Cameroonian ID and a Nigerian accent. My mother lives in Cameroon."

"I'm sorry—I don't have space here."

"They told me your dog died, and I might be able to stay where he stayed."

"In the room on the side of the house? There's no bed in there, and it's full of things in storage."

"I don't mind. It's better than sleeping outside."

She glanced over at Daniel's book on the table, wondering if this man was here to help her. He was standing at the door looking around, waiting for Jessie's reply. After a few seconds, she looked back at him and smiled.

"Can you take me to the Abuja airport?"

Excited, the man slapped his hands together. "Of course. That's where I'm going."

"Great. I need a few days to get ready, and then we go. Can you get some water from the well?"

"Sure. I can do that."

Jessie shared her dinner with him. In the course of their conversation, Nathaniel told her that he was a sixth-degree black belt in karate. How strange, she thought, that he would practice martial arts, and be ranked higher than her sensei.

After dinner, he retired to his room, and Jessie locked up the house. Exhausted from her long trip, she went straight to bed.

She woke up early in the morning.

I had another dream. It was dark, and I was hovering over the water. Something boomed, and then I saw the reflection of a man. It looked like Daniel. Within a few moments, something pierced my heart and took away all my pain. I was shooting across the sky. What an incredible feeling! Was it love?

When Jessie opened the front door, Nathaniel was sitting on the porch. She invited him in for breakfast, and he told her about a dream he'd had; he'd seen her face in a shooting star. Another strange coincidence, she thought, feeling a bit leery.

After breakfast, Nathaniel went into town and Jessie headed to work, where she told the doctor that she would be going away on vacation for at least a month. Knowing that the doctor was from France, she nonchalantly probed for his thoughts about his country. He didn't like it, he told her; there were too many fake people there.

When Nathaniel walked into the house after work, Jessie was making dinner.

"Did you have a nice day?" she asked.

"Yes—I went to town for a while, and then to a field to meditate and practice karate."

"Good. I bet you're ready to get back home."

"Yes, I miss Nigeria. So where are you going from the Abuja airport, anyway?"

Jessie felt nervous. "Home," she lied. "For vacation." She didn't want anyone to know.

"Why? You don't like Africa?"

"No, I like it here."

"You're not very convincing."

"Don't get me wrong—I really like it here. If there's anything I don't like, it's the black magic and witchcraft."

Nathaniel laughed. "It's not bad. People just don't know how to use it."

Jessie shrugged.

"One of my brothers died," he said. "They cut his body into pieces and boiled it with special herbs. While we were chanting, he came back to life, and now he lives in Nigeria with his wives and children."

"What kind of grotesque process is that?"

Nathaniel chuckled. "It's the process of eternal life," he said.

Jessie's stomach clenched, but she had to know more. "Nathaniel, this is all very strange. Who are you, really? And how did you get here?"

He hesitated and then took a deep breath.

"Not to scare you, but I used to deal in drugs. All my business went bad, and I was locked up in prison for over a month with nothing to eat and only water to drink. The only help I got was from the Satanic Church; otherwise I'd probably be dead."

Jessie looked terrified.

"Don't worry. I'm not dangerous. I'm more like the prodigal son going back to my real father."

Jessie closed her eyes, praying silently, and in that moment he kissed her. His lips were cold. She pulled away, focusing her mind on Daniel, her light and hope. It was clear that she had to go as soon as possible.

"I have a boyfriend—sorry."

"Oh! I didn't know. I'm the one who should be sorry. Who is he? What's his name?"

Jessie searched her mind for an answer.

"Eddie—he lives in the States. That's one reason I'm going home."

Nathaniel kept probing for more information, so Jessie told him she was tired and wanted to go to bed early.

In the morning another envelope had been pushed under her door. This time it bore no return address or postmark, and she felt a chill when she held it. She opened it reluctantly.

Dear Jessie,

Do you think you can escape me? My demons and I (the paramount ruler of hell) have come to claim your soul.

First, we will skin you alive. Then we will tear your flesh into pieces to give you a taste of the suffering that awaits you. You will wander in my kingdom forever, world without end.

Your sufferings can be lessened on the condition that you become one of my numerous sweethearts, for I'm as lecherous as a he-goat.

Forever,
The Prince of Darkness

Jessie was petrified. She was sure the letter was from Nathaniel. After he'd gone into town, she crept into his room and found some paper that he'd written on. The handwriting matched.

There were no phones in her village; the nearest was in Bankim, two hours away by taxi. She got a cab there and called the Peace Corps Office, explaining about all the strange things that had happened to her, including the letter under her door. They told her to come in, but she insisted that she had to go home. Her father was sick, she said, and she needed medical leave. After haggling with them, they gave her a twelve-week leave of absence, the maximum allowed under the Family and Medical Leave Act; they would investigate while she was gone.

It was dark by the time she returned, and Nathaniel's door was shut. Quietly she slipped into her house, locking the door behind her. After filling her backpack with only her most precious belongings, she went to sleep.

That night, in the fog of her dream, snakes surrounded her, hissing hysterically and glaring at her with their evil eyes. The ancient book appeared in the sky, and she soared up into it. There was light everywhere, and Daniel was inside.

Before sunrise she got dressed, looked over the house one more time for anything she might have forgotten, and grabbed her backpack. She slipped out, locked the door behind her, and started jogging to Atta. After about forty-five minutes she was breathing heavily, but still moving as quickly as she could.

In Atta, she ate some bananas and asked a stranger how to get to Abuja. He referred her to someone else, who referred her to another person. Finally someone told her to cross the border by foot and get a taxi to the next town. From there, she could find a bus. It would take her the rest of the day.

With great determination, Jessie set out. She would spend the night in Abuja and leave the next morning, if there were any flights.

9
Reunited

Jessie flagged down a taxi to the airport. Clutching a ticket bought on the Internet, she began to push through a large crowd of people. Several officers were looking around, randomly scanning and searching luggage. One of them approached Jessie and opened her bag. "You cannot take ebony out of the country without a permit. Remove the item from your bag, please."

"Where am I supposed to put it?" Jessie panicked.

"That's your problem, ma'am, but the ebony cannot leave the country."

The officer went on checking other people's bags, while Jessie stood there, paralyzed. She had put Daniel's book in an ebony box to protect it, and she was afraid to take it out now in front of all of these people. Perhaps he would forget about her and let it go . . .

After checking a few more people, the officer came back to Jessie. He looked annoyed. "I told you to take the ebony out of your bag. Give me your documents now."

Nervously, Jessie gave the officer her passport, forgetting that she had put all her cash in the back. Thinking it was a pay-off, he took it out carefully, then handed back her documents and motioned her forward.

Wait! That's all my money!

Just before he pocketed the cash, she took back a few small bills, rubbing her belly as if she was hungry. When the officer didn't respond, Jessie made her way through the rest of security to the gate and sat down, relieved. In a short time they boarded the plane.

The flight from Abuja to Nice was about ten hours. With a deep sigh, Jessie fell into her seat and stared out the window, remembering the moment when she first heard Daniel's voice—emotional, spiritual, almost mystical. He couldn't have stolen the book; there had to be some logical explanation.

She ran through her connection in Frankfurt, her eyes gritty from lack of sleep. On the next plane she sat by an old couple who held hands, leaning against each other as they slept.

Jessie thought about her relationship with Daniel and what she wanted it to become. She wouldn't tell him about the tarantula divination, the mysterious messages in her journal, or her past experiences, she decided. It was important to start fresh. She would only tell him about the threatening letter under her door.

Finally they landed at the Nice Côte d'Azur airport. Daniel had told her to wait for him in the main terminal when she called him from Abuja with her flight information.

There were lots of people waiting near the exit, some holding up signs. Jessie looked around eagerly for Daniel's face. Having pictured herself running into his arms, being spun around and kissed passionately, she was disappointed that he was late.

Her stomach was growling, and the smell of hot crepes made her salivate, so she tried to change the little cash she had left at a kiosk, but they didn't accept CFA francs. Her money was worthless.

The voice came magically, unexpectedly, from behind her. "Jessie?"

She turned around. Daniel was smiling, his arms open. It wasn't exactly the way she'd imagined it. He didn't spin her around; they just hugged and kissed.

"Thank God you're here," he said. "Let's go."

Daniel walked quickly to a black BMW in short-term parking. Jessie followed with her backpack, threw it in the back, and got in beside him. As he was pulling out of the lot, his phone rang.

At first he listened quietly, but suddenly his face turned red, and he started yelling in what sounded like Italian. It sounded as if he was angry. Abruptly he hung up and took a deep breath.

"You seem tired," he said, his voice softer.

"Yes," replied Jessie. "It was a long trip. Are you okay?"

"Oh, I'm fine. People are always taking advantage, and it makes me angry."

"Why, what's going on?"

"A dealer wants to sell me a manuscript for a lot more than it's worth. Anyway, you should sleep for a while."

His eyes on the road and one hand on the steering wheel, he reached into the backseat to find a pillow, but Jessie stopped him. "Actually, I'm hungry. Can we get something to eat?"

"Of course. There's a nice restaurant not too far from here, with very good food."

In the restaurant, Jessie was quiet. Daniel was charming and gregarious. The waiter gave him recommendations, and he ordered a variety of dishes.

"So I have some explaining to do," he said with a chuckle. "First, I didn't steal the book, as you suggested in your letter. It belongs to me. It was passed down through generations to my father. I brought it with me to the summit for a presentation I was giving."

"So why do you think it was reported as stolen in the newspaper?"

"After my presentation on uncovering ancient wisdom for a better world, I was offered a lot of money for the book, which I refused. Then I found my room ransacked."

Daniel paused to sip the wine. He nodded his approval to the waiter, who poured them each a glass.

"Anyway, I was right to give it to you, because I was searched at the airport from head to toe," he said. "Whoever wants this book is very important, and has connections."

Jessie nodded. "I know it's important," she said, "but it's not really a book, is it? It contains no symbols or words."

"Yes, it is a book—a sacred book."

"How do you read it?"

"I don't know, but the language is in the sound."

"I figured that out when my pendant struck one of the pages. What a lovely sound it makes."

Daniel sipped his wine and looked around casually to see if anyone was listening. "Actually, it always makes a sound when it's open," he whispered. "You just don't know it, because it's outside the range of human hearing."

Jessie remembered the cat's response to the book; maybe it had heard the sound she couldn't hear. Rami had never been near the open book, or he might have heard it also.

"If I'm right," he said, "it's written in divine language."

"The Word?"

"How did you know?"

"In the beginning was the Word," said Jessie. "It was with God, and it was God. It's the only divine language I can fathom."

Daniel found Jessie's hand on the table and caressed it with his fingers. He was smiling, and he looked happy. Moving up from his chair, he leaned over and softly kissed her mouth.

"When I first saw you lying on that cotton pile all by yourself, I knew you were the one for me," he said. "We can change the world together."

Jessie smiled warmly. The waiter was coming with a plate of all kinds of grilled seafood, and another of roast potatoes and green salad. They both grabbed their forks. Jessie dug in eagerly.

"I guess you were hungry!" said Daniel.

"Starving is more like it," she said, grinning.

With her belly full, Jessie fell asleep in the car, only waking when, after an hour's drive, they arrived. Daniel parked the car in front of an arduous, narrow stairway. Jessie grabbed her bag and followed him up the steps. Flowers and foliage were everywhere. A chameleon scurried across the wall as Daniel unlocked the gate.

About twenty steps through the gate was an ancient tower. Behind them was a village by the sea. To one side a valley stretched out below them, full of meadow flowers and scattered trees; beyond it rose a lush, green mountainside.

"Spectacular! Breathtaking! Where are we?"

"This is our home. Do you like it?"

Our home? His and mine? Jessie thought. Was he serious?

She went out onto a balcony. Cactuses and all kinds of bushes and flowers covered the hillside below, and hummingbirds zipped in and out of tall flowerpots sitting majestically on the wall enclosing the balcony.

"It's like a dream," she said, looking toward the sea. She knew this was the French Riviera, but it felt like paradise. For a moment she wondered if she was still alive, still Jessie, living in the world.

Daniel pulled her close and touched her lips with his finger. A cool breeze passed over their faces as he kissed her. Jessie had never felt this close, so connected—and to someone she hardly knew.

In the house, Daniel showed her around. The floors and walls were stone. A wood-plank ceiling was supported by dark ancient beams. The air smelled faintly of incense, like an ancient church. All the furniture was from the sixteenth century or before. Old manuscripts and antiques were everywhere; it looked like a museum. Jessie was stunned.

"How old is this place?"

"About a thousand years," replied Daniel.

"Are you some kind of antiquarian or something?"

"As a matter of fact, I am," he said proudly.

They sat down next to each other on the bed. After a few moments of silence, Daniel got up and turned on some classical music. Then he kissed Jessie's neck and moved his hand to her back and down. Before Jessie could ask him another question, he had completely undressed her. As modest as she was, it felt right.

She unclothed him, and they continued to explore each other's bodies, with a passion that left them speechless and drove deep into Jessie's heart. Like her dream, she could feel him piercing her with light and sending her on a journey into the stars. He pressed himself against her, but then stopped abruptly, a strange, ominous expression crossing his face.

"What's wrong?" she asked.

"I can't."

"Don't worry, it's okay."

"I can't, until you know . . . that I am married."

Jessie pulled away from him. Her heart sank into her stomach, and she felt like she was going to vomit.

"I'm sorry I didn't tell you before. We haven't been intimate in more than twenty years."

Jessie was silent. Trembling, she turned around and curled up into fetal position, as if she were trying to protect herself from something unknown.

Daniel embraced her from behind. "My dear, people get married for all kinds of reasons. She wanted security, and I wanted my freedom. We both wanted to have a child, and we made a good team."

Jessie turned back around. "What do you mean, you wanted your freedom?"

Daniel looked away. "Dorothy let me do what I wanted as long as I didn't tell her. And, well, I did . . . before I met you."

"Do you mean with other women?"

"Yes," he said, shamefaced. "But it was just attraction, infatuation, not real love like this."

"How do you know that you really love me? And that I really love you?"

"For one, it feels like we've known each other forever. And our connection is much deeper than physical."

"So are you going to get a divorce and ask me to marry you?" Jessie asked sarcastically. "You're that sure that you really love me?"

He smiled and looked over her face as if he were trying to read her. Jessie held her tongue and waited for his reply, wondering whether he would be honest, or just tell her what she wanted to hear.

"No, I can't get a divorce. It wouldn't be fair for me to leave her."

Nervous and confused, Jessie took a deep breath and sighed.

Then she put her hand on his cheek. "Daniel, what do you really want from me?"

Before he could reply, she said, "Tell me the truth. Do you really love me? Or do you just like something about me, and you're using love as an excuse to get what you really want? Be honest, please."

Daniel wrinkled his forehead. "Look, marriage is something we do in *law*, in culture. Few people get it right. You and me, we have the real *love*. We know it. We can give our souls to each other and fly. And we will generate—"

Jessie put her fingers on his lips and followed with a slow kiss. She closed her eyes to savor him without distraction. "I understand. I feel it, too. Let's go on."

When the sun rose, Daniel and Jessie were still making love.

Abruptly Jessie stopped. "Daniel?"

"Yes, my dear?"

"Are we in heaven? I've never felt this way before. It's incredible. I can go on forever . . . after we sleep awhile."

He grinned, and then his phone rang abruptly.

Jessie got up, putting on Daniel's robe. She went to the kitchen and checked the refrigerator. There was no food, so she opened the cabinet and made them both some tea. Then she sat down on the living room couch. On the coffee table was an open book, full of ancient symbols, with Latin descriptions of their meaning. Daniel was hungry for knowledge, she could see.

After he'd finished his phone conversation, Daniel sat down next to Jessie, sipping his tea.

"Who was that?" she asked.

"Nobody important," he said. "Do you like this book?"

"Yes, I've always been fascinated with symbolism."

Daniel caressed the parchment with his hand lovingly. "This is four hundred years old . . . quite rare. And if you like it, I would like to give it to you."

Jessie was overwhelmed with gratitude.

"No, I can't accept such a precious gift," she replied.

"If you don't, you will offend me. Anyway, whatever is mine is yours. That's how sure I am about you and our love. Believe me, I've had a lot of experience, and I know beyond any doubt that what we have is different."

"Well, thank you for your confidence in me."

Daniel took Jessie for a walk down by the sea. The sky was clear, and it was a beautiful sunny day. A wind came from the water, blowing their hair around.

"Do you smell that?" asked Daniel.

Jessie took a big whiff. "Smells like fish."

"It smells like Sunday to me."

Fishermen were coming in with their boats. Daniel and Jessie crossed the street and walked down a quieter sidewalk, away from the wind and water.

"Do you smell the flowers on the graves?"

"Oh, yes . . . only on Sunday," replied Jessie.

"Take a whiff of that homemade bread."

"And the incense from the church."

"Roasted chestnuts."

"Coffee cake. Yum."

"Grilled salmon."

"Garbage . . . yuck!"

They stopped in a café for lunch. The waiter gave them menus. Browsing through, Jessie told Daniel that she would like some kind of fish, and he ordered for them both.

"So tell me more about you and your life," she said.

Daniel put his hand over her wrist and rubbed her skin with his thumb. His eyes were bright; he was smiling.

"When I was young, I went to a convent because I didn't like the world. It was a lonely place, without love, and without God, really. So I left and started studying the divine on my own, mostly through ancient manuscripts and religious texts."

"And you made a living like this?"

"Yes. After a decade of translating and reading, I wanted to use my knowledge to help humanity evolve. Different organizations funded my research for different reasons, and I became a pretty good antiquarian too."

The waiter brought them each a bowl of bouillabaisse, a Provençal fish stew.

"This looks so good!" said Jessie.

"I bet you're hungry after last night."

Jessie grinned and passed the bread. "Why do you call God 'the divine'?" she asked. "I'm just curious, because it's not very common."

Daniel slapped a mosquito on his arm. "God is man's idea of the divine, warped through history. The divine is free of gender and religious connotations."

"Do you really think the divine talks to us?"

"Of course! The problem is, we don't listen."

"Honestly, how can we listen when we don't understand the language?"

"With our hearts. The divine language is not a language of words; it's a language of feeling."

"But feelings originate in the brain," she said, "and are driven by beliefs and thoughts. That's a scientific fact."

"Actually, the divine language that I'm talking about moves through your heart," replied Daniel. "If you stop thinking, you can feel it."

Jessie wrinkled her brow. "Then why do we listen to ministers, priests, and rabbis? Why do we read religious and sacred books to move our minds?"

"We move our minds because we want to feel; we live for feeling! Human language, artistic expressions, both become thoughts and beliefs that generate all kinds of feelings in our lives."

"Wait a minute, there are *two* sources of feeling? You just said that both the heart and brain create feelings. That doesn't make any sense."

"I said the real divine language speaks through the heart. The brain is supposed to interpret the meaning and respond cooperatively."

"And why doesn't it?"

"Because it has been trained to rule, not respond. It oppresses the heart and stops the natural divine flow in our lives. It creates its own pseudo feelings."

Jessie saw the brain-heart relationship like man and woman. Man yearned for power like the brain, and woman desired union like the heart. Part of it was physical, hormonal, but it was more than that. *What is physical is also spiritual. They are two sides of the same thing.*

"So the heart has two purposes: a physical one, to pump blood, a spiritual one, the divine."

"Yes, divine communication. Your heart is your spiritual ear and voice box," said Daniel. "We've known this for centuries."

The waiter brought a bottle of red wine, and had begun pouring when someone bumped into him from behind. A few drops splashed onto Daniel's shirt. He scowled and spoke angrily to the waiter, who apologized profusely as he tried to clean up the mess. Daniel sent him away, wiping at his shirt with a wet napkin to little effect.

Jessie was shocked by the impetuous change in Daniel's demeanor, but she didn't say anything.

"Anyway, back to our conversation," said Daniel. "Did you know that the heart is the first organ that forms in the body? From one minute to the next, it just starts beating. Nobody knows how; it's a mystery."

"I always thought the brain was responsible for starting the heart."

"That's not all; the heart thinks and remembers too. Did you know there are neurons in the heart?"

"Really?"

"Yes, about forty thousand. In the case of heart transplants, recipients have developed some of the same hobbies and interests that their donors had. This is science!"

Jessie was amazed. She had never thought to question what she'd learned in school: that the heart was just a muscle.

After lunch, they continued their walk, meandering to the beach and lying down on the sand. Their bellies full, they gazed silently at the sea, listening to the waves crashing on the shore.

"Look there," Daniel said abruptly, pointing. "Look into the orange and red, between the day and night. Do you see it?"

Jessie stared at the sky above the horizon for a moment. "I think so."

"That's the divine. Can you feel it?"

"It does give me a beautiful feeling."

"And what does that feeling do to you?"

"It inspires me, gives me hope and purpose."

"That's the divine language flowing through your heart, collaborating with your mind harmonically."

They watched a crab digging itself into the sand until it disappeared, and then lay gazing at each other. When the sun had almost set and the mosquitoes started feeding, they ran home.

10
Nicholas Flamel

J essie woke up in a cold sweat, dreaming again of the boy from the sea; this time he was drowning, and she was swimming toward him. She got abruptly out of bed and went to the window. Lightning flashed, and thunder cracked. It was pouring. She got back in bed and opened her journal. Daniel was still asleep.

Looking for inspiration, she turned on some music, Luciano Pavarotti, softly. Then she wrapped her arms tightly around Daniel's slumbering form and listened; he was snoring, out of sync with the music. She kissed his cheek and turned around to write.

I'm listening now with my heart, like you told me to do. Did you lead me here? Is Daniel my soul mate? I think I'm in love. Actually, I know I'm in love. So please don't go away, and keep talking to me. I want to know more.

About twenty minutes later, Daniel woke up. He started speaking to Jessie, but she was in deep thought, writing, and didn't reply. So he went to take a hot bath. The music relaxed him as he soaked in the water. When the aria "Ave Maria" opened, he started singing in Italian.

Jessie heard him in the background and smiled—he sounded just like Pavarotti. But she was still deep in thought, penning her journal.

If you are the Word, then tell me more about what you do and how you created everything in the universe. I really don't understand how "something" came from "nothing" with such order. I want to understand.

Daniel finished his bath and came out, singing boisterously. He was trying to be funny in his way, dancing around the room, looking for something to wear. Jessie smiled, but didn't pay him much attention, as she was still trying to put down her thoughts.

"My Jessie, you are so beautiful, lying there, writing about me and our love," Daniel said jokingly.

Jessie still didn't reply, so he walked over and lifted her chin with his finger. She looked up with tender, affectionate eyes. "Good morning, my love," she said sweetly. "I'm sorry—I just finished."

"That's more like it," said Daniel. "You are such a serious writer, so focused and committed to your words."

In his underwear, he fumbled through his CDs, looking for something else, and finally put on the Bee Gees' "Stayin' Alive." Then he pulled Jessie up, and they danced together, around each other, all over the room. She threw off her pajamas and pushed him down onto the bed.

"It seems that music inspires more in you than just writing,"

Daniel said, grabbing her and rolling over. "I like this!" Jessie grinned and pushed him away playfully.

"Daniel, I was thinking . . . If the Word moves things with sound, and the Word is a language of feeling, how are sound and feeling connected?"

Daniel put his hand on her cheek. "Good question. If the bones in your hand move, and the skin on your hand feels, how are they connected?"

Jessie laughed, mouth open. "What a ridiculous question."

"My point exactly. We're all living among the same planets, which rotate around the same sun, in the same rhythm, under the same stars. It's all one big body."

"You have all the answers, don't you?"

"No—we still have much to learn."

Abruptly the phone rang. When Daniel answered, his mood changed. His face reddened, and he screamed at the person on the line. Then he hung up and slammed the phone down on the bed.

"I'm sorry, but I have to go. I'll be back in a few days."

"What's wrong, Daniel? Why were you so upset?"

"My wife is sick, and the doctors have been making too many mistakes."

"Is it lifethreatening?"

"I don't think so," he replied. "I'm just tired. I want to stay here with you." He handed her a mobile phone, some cash, and a credit card on his way out the door. "I'm sorry again. Call me if you need anything."

Jessie wondered why he hadn't kissed her good-bye. Two minutes later, he ran back in and gave her a big kiss.

"I forgot . . ."

Nervous about his running off to his wife, and wondering what to do with herself, Jessie found Daniel's library. Her eyes moved from medieval boxes to age-old paintings stacked against the wall. Papers were piled up everywhere; it was a mess. Jessie moved closer to read a scroll that hung beside Daniel's desk:

Nigredo (black)
Self and its complexity
The fertile darkness

Albedo (white)
The divine spark inside
Prima materia, seed

Rubedo (red)
Love and harmony
Transmutation

Red was the color in the sunset, she thought, wondering if this was some kind of religion. A built-in bookcase ran across the entire back wall, full of old books and manuscripts. She opened a few, but they were written in Latin and other languages that she didn't understand. So she walked around the house some more, bored and lonely.

She wanted to go somewhere, somewhere artsy and full of culture. Spontaneously, she booked a hotel on the Internet and bought a train ticket to Paris. She took a bus to the station in Avignon, and by midafternoon she was walking past chic cafés, elegant shops, and parks everywhere. Strolling around, she stumbled upon the Louvre.

Inside the museum, Jessie found herself captivated by a massive painting of a naked man lying on his back, glowing white against the dark all around him, a single ray of light rising from his abdomen toward the sky. The painting was by Anselm

Kiefer, and it was called *Nigredo, Albedo, Rubedo*: the three colors of alchemy, like the scroll on Daniel's wall.

"Do you like it?" a voice asked.

Jessie trembled and looked behind her. An older woman with salt-and-pepper hair stood there. "Sorry, were you talking to me?"

"Yes, I saw you here a while ago. You've been staring at that painting for a long time."

"Oh, I'm just trying to understand. I thought alchemy was about turning lead into gold."

"That's one goal, to create the perfect metal, but the other goal is to achieve the perfect life—a life without death."

"So it's a religion?" said Jessie. "A path to perfection in both the mineral and human kingdoms?"

"You got it. Haven't you heard of Nicholas Flamel? He was the greatest alchemist in all Europe. They say he succeeded in making both gold and the elixir of life in the fourteenth century."

"Really? Do you believe it?"

"Gold, yes. How else would a small bookseller become so wealthy? Honestly, I don't know about the elixir."

"Are you talking about the legendary substance that prolongs life indefinitely?"

"Yes, the elixir of life. Since he'd made it, Flamel wasn't supposed to die, but he carved his own tombstone."

"You're right—no one expecting immortality would carve his own tombstone. So did he actually die or not?"

"His death was recorded in 1418, but his tomb is empty. Some people think that thieves stole his body, but he has been spotted throughout the centuries. There is no proof of anything."

"Where is his tombstone?"

"It's on display at the Musée de Cluny."

"Thanks—I'll try to go there."

"You should enjoy the Louvre first, though; there's so much to see."

Strange, Jessie thought; *I did not stop at the Mona Lisa, or any of the other famous paintings here. Something brought me to this painting, this place, this moment.*

After walking around the museum for a while, she went out to find something to eat. She bought a crepe from a street vendor and wandered around until she came upon a small, quaint bookstore.

"Excuse me," Jessie said to a clerk. "I'm looking for a book about Nicholas Flamel."

He took her to the children's section and pulled a book off the shelf. Jessie looked it over and shook her head no.

"I'm looking for something more historical, factual."

"Just down the street, there's a churchyard with some of Flamel's mysterious ciphers," said the clerk, "and there are several books for sale inside the church."

Jessie left the bookstore and found the churchyard. She looked over the mysterious symbols and picked up a brochure, intrigued:

He dreamed of an angel, radiant and winged, who held a book in his hands. "Look well at this book, Nicholas," the angel told him. "At first you will understand nothing in it, neither you nor any other man. But one day you will see in it that which no other man will be able to see."

Sure enough, one day a stranger in need of money appeared in Flamel's bookstore to sell a manuscript. Recognizing it as the book from his dream, he bought it without bargaining. After studying the book, it is said that he learned how to make gold and the elixir.

Suddenly Jessie's phone rang. She fumbled around her bag to find it. It was Daniel.

"Hello."

"Jessie, where are you?"

"I'm in Paris. And you?"

"Paris! Who are you with?"

"I'm alone. I just couldn't stay home by myself. It was too quiet, and there was nothing to do."

"You could have walked down by the sea. Paris is so far."

"Yes, but I've always wanted to see Paris. I'm sure you've been here many times, anyway."

"Okay . . . Well, things didn't take as long as I thought they would. I'm coming to find you."

"Is your wife okay?" asked Jessie.

"So-so. I took her to another doctor."

Daniel arrived late that night and found Jessie at the hotel. Exhausted, he fell into bed with a newspaper.

"So what did the doctor say?"

"I don't know. She's just not well."

"What kind of symptoms does she have?"

He wasn't listening; his mind was somewhere else. When he didn't answer, Jessie asked him again. Then she waved her hand in front of his face. Daniel looked at her with bloodshot eyes.

"Can't you see I'm tired?" he snapped. "I drove home to find you, and then I drove here! I need to relax now."

"Okay, sorry." Jessie was hurt by his tone, but she didn't say so.

In the middle of the night Jessie woke up, squinting. The light was on, and Daniel was reading. As soon as he saw Jessie move, he grabbed her and pulled her close to him. Before she could open her eyes, he was on top of her.

"I've never met a woman like you before. Where have you been all my life?"

"Can you turn off the light?" Jessie mumbled.

"No—I need to see you."

"Why do men have to see a woman to love her?"

"It's balance, my dear."

"And the man who is blind?"

"I cannot imagine." Daniel chuckled. "He would experience a different balance, I guess."

In the morning Jessie and Daniel got up late and went to breakfast. Jessie ordered a coffee, but Daniel changed her order to green tea.

"Coffee is bad for you," he said. "You have to take care of yourself now . . . and listen to me."

"Okay—thanks for looking out for me."

"Of course! You are my love."

Jessie was happy. No man had ever expressed a desire to take care of her before.

"What would you like to do today?" he asked.

"Can we go to the Musée de Cluny?"

"Why? What do you want to see?"

"The tombstone of Nicholas Flamel."

Daniel's face turned pale.

"Flamel!" he replied. "You know about him?"

"A woman in the Louvre told me . . . Are you all right?"

"Fine! Okay, we'll go. I just didn't know you were interested in that kind of stuff."

They checked out of the hotel and put their things in Daniel's car, then started walking.

"What do you know about Flamel?" asked Jessie.

"He was a great alchemist from France."

"What I don't understand is why he carved his own tombstone, when he wasn't expecting to die."

"Oh, but he was expecting to die. It's impossible to go on in the same body forever."

"So what is the elixir that he created?"

"You're right—in mythology, it's a legendary substance for making gold and prolonging life indefinitely. But the real *spiritual* elixir is transmutation."

"Do you mean reincarnation?"

"No. Can you imagine becoming a cockroach after you were a human?"

Jessie chuckled. "So tell me what you mean."

"Transmutation involves intelligence and feeling. It's the path to the divine, where we find the real eternal life and the gold of all consciousness."

"Ah, so physical gold represents a spiritual gold, two sides of the same thing," she said.

"As above, so below."

Daniel pulled out two small glass vials from his shirt pocket. Then he broke off the top of one of them, and drank the liquid in it. He broke the top off the other and handed it to Jessie.

"What's that?" asked Jessie.

"Homeopathic medicine."

"For what?"

"For a long, healthy life."

Jessie drank the liquid. It had a salty, metallic taste.

"If the divine is so much better, then why do we try to hang on to our lives as long as possible?"

"Because we can feel here," Daniel said.

"There's no feeling in the divine?"

"We don't know! I think we need bodies to feel, but every

feeling has an intelligence behind it, and I think we become a part of that intelligence when we die."

"But if intelligence drives feeling, then what drives intelligence?"

"Maybe feeling also. That's why we're all afraid to die; we can't project or understand the experience."

"It's hard to imagine any consciousness without feeling. Even when we sleep, we feel through our dreams."

After about forty-five minutes, they found the Musée de Cluny. There weren't many people, and they quickly located the tombstone of Nicholas Flamel. Various figures were carved on the stone and, at the center, a closed book under a key and a sun.

"What do you think it means?" asked Jessie.

"That he found the path to the divine, hidden in his book. He found the spiritual elixir."

After walking through the museum, they went back to the car and headed home. Daniel was quieter than usual, and he looked tired.

Jessie was thinking about the scroll on his wall and the painting at the Louvre. "Daniel, what is the spiritual meaning of *nigredo, albedo, rubedo*? I know it means 'black, white, red,' and it's a symbolic path to harmony, but I don't understand what color has to do with this process, and why it ends with redness."

"Color symbolism is an important part of alchemy. The changes in color represent the successive transmutation I was telling you about. Red is the color of blood, symbolizing the union of male and female and the resurrection."

Daniel seemed to know a lot about Nicholas Flamel and the spiritual side of alchemy, Jessie thought. "Daniel, I don't know how else to ask, so I'm just going to come out with it. Are you an alchemist?"

Daniel's jaw dropped, and his eyes got big.

"How did you know?"

"So you are?"

"Yes!"

"Why didn't you tell me before?"

"I was going to tell you at the right time."

"Do you know how to make gold?"

"Yes, but it's a very difficult process."

"Do you know how to achieve the real eternal life?"

"I'm working on it. This is why we have to understand the ancient book. I think the answer is there," Daniel said, pulling over the car.

"What are you doing?" asked Jessie.

"Something very important."

After he'd parked on the side of the road, he leaned over and kissed Jessie passionately for a long time. "You are the one for me. No doubt! But I want you to promise me something."

"What?"

"To be faithful to me forever."

"Yes, I promise!"

He smiled and started the car again.

"Wait . . . aren't you going to promise *me*?"

"What?" he said, grinning.

"To be faithful! It goes both ways."

He laughed. "Of course!"

Jessie grabbed his hand and put it on the inside of her leg. He squeezed her leg and growled. He kept looking at her, taking his eyes off the road, and Jessie began to get nervous.

"Okay, please watch the road, not me. So what are we doing tomorrow?"

"We have to start studying the ancient book," he said. "We have to research the sound it makes to understand the meaning."

As soon as they got home, Daniel's phone rang. He answered and went to the other room while Jessie unpacked her bag. When he returned, he looked frustrated. "I have to go again. I'm sorry. I'll be back soon."

"Again? What's going on?"

"It's my wife. She needs my help."

"Oh, okay. Where does she think you are all the time, anyway? You must have a reason for being away so much."

"She thinks I'm traveling for work, doing research. She doesn't know about you."

"Are you going to keep me a secret forever?"

"As I told you, she doesn't want to know."

"What kind of relationship is that, not to care about what your husband is doing?"

"She's sick, too, and I don't want to give her any more stress. I'm sure you can understand."

"Do you love her?"

"I really have to go."

"Can I go with you?"

"No, but when I get back, we're going to start studying the ancient book. So be prepared."

He kissed her on the lips and ran out the door. Unhappily, Jessie wondered if he was being straight with her.

Daniel is good to help his wife. Not many men would do this, but there's something about him that scares me. Where is this fear coming from? From jealousy? Insecurity? The Word? Is it an obstacle or a warning?

11
The Research

A coin bounced off the table and landed on the floor. Jessie and Daniel were at the hospital, observing how patients responded to the sounds of the ancient book. Nurses walked to and from the room. Another coin landed on the page, and it chimed.

Jessie was reviewing the data they'd recorded, trying to recognize patterns among the patients they were working with. Some showed signs of healing, others were the same, and some were worse than before.

"There's no definite relationship between hearing the sounds and healing," she said.

"That's not encouraging," replied Daniel. "Okay, let's check back with our patients one more time next week, just to make sure. Are you ready to go?"

"Yes, I'm exhausted."

"Me, too. It's been a long day."

Daniel and Jessie said good-bye to the nurses and left the

hospital. As they were walking down the street, a deep, scratchy voice called out behind them, "That's a nice book you have."

They both turned around. A man in a dirty black raincoat stood crookedly, a bottle in his hand, smiling from ear to ear. Jessie tensed up.

"You were at the homeless shelter the other day," said Daniel, a smirk on his face.

Jessie remembered. They were testing the book to see if it gave hope to people who had lost everything. This particular man had laughed hysterically every time the book chimed.

"We don't get many visitors. Anyway, thanks for coming. You made me feel better," said the man.

"In what way?" asked Daniel.

"Ha! I don't remember. Can you imagine that?" He stumbled over his own foot, and Daniel caught him before he fell. His breath smelled like whiskey. They had started walking away when suddenly the man grabbed Jessie's shoulder.

"Let me tell you something," he said.

With a scowl on his face, Daniel pushed the man away from Jessie.

"Tell *me*, sir, and don't touch her," he said forcefully.

The man stumbled backward. Jessie didn't say anything; she liked that Daniel was protective of her. As they started walking away again, the man hollered something with a shaky voice. Telling Jessie to wait, Daniel stepped back toward him.

"Excuse me?" he said.

"I said, make music if you want a better show."

"It isn't a show!" screamed Daniel. "Go screw yourself, mister. Get a life, and do something with it!"

"I'll do that! You too!"

"*Au revoir* and *bon nuit*," whispered Daniel under his breath, and walked away quickly, tugging Jessie behind him.

When the man was out of sight, Jessie elbowed Daniel. "You know, he's just a poor drunk trying to be helpful in his own way. You didn't have to get so angry."

"Bah, it's people like him who make the world filthy. We have to live in this world, you know."

It was obvious that Daniel was very tense. Jessie wanted him to see things differently, so he could calm down. "I kind of like the idea of making our research more attractive," she said. "He has a good point. Don't you think?"

"Come on, Jessie. You're not Mary Poppins, and I'm not the chimney sweep," he said, only half joking. "Or would you rather go on Broadway than change the world?"

"Broadway, for sure." Jessie laughed.

Daniel scowled playfully.

That night they lay in bed, reading the newspaper together.

"Daniel?"

"Yes, Jessie?"

"Let's go to the beach tomorrow."

"Good idea, my dear. We haven't tested the book with ordinary people."

"I didn't mean to work. I'm tired. I just want to relax and swim, maybe read a good book."

"We have to keep working, or we're never going to understand the book."

"Listen, we've been to health facilities, homeless shelters, prisons, schools. We've tested the sound everywhere, but we're not getting any closer."

"That's why we need to go to the beach."

"Don't you understand? They think we're crazy!"

"I can't relax until we find some answers."

Jessie sighed. "Have you thought that maybe it's a sacred book of love, to help soul mates find each other?"

"Yes, of course. The Word, the language of the divine, leads to love. For sure it brought us together, because its nature is love. But there's a reason."

"Love isn't reason enough?"

"Not in our case. You and I have to understand how to achieve love, so we can use it to change the world. That's what I think is in the book."

Jessie sighed and opened her journal.

I love Daniel, but he's making me a little crazy, doing everything his way. He doesn't understand the more subtle ways that we can change the world through the feelings we have for each other.

In the morning, Jessie put on her bathing suit. But when Daniel saw her, he passionately took it right back off, and pulled her back into bed.

Later, after a late breakfast, they went to the beach and sat down near the entrance, on a sheet. When people walked by, Jessie dropped coins on the open book, and Daniel called them over to talk.

Most people ignored them, but a young man with long stringy hair and a Speedo stopped by.

"So are you guys like fortune-tellers or something?"

"No, we're studying the effect of sounds on people's thoughts, feelings, and behaviors," replied Daniel.

"Why, dude?"

Daniel looked to Jessie for help. "So we can understand," she said, knowing that it sounded stupid.

The young man looked dubious. "Oh, okay . . . Good luck, guys."

"Daniel, we do look rather ridiculous," said Jessie. "Maybe we need to be more entertaining and less serious."

Daniel smiled reluctantly and stood up. "Ladies and gentlemen, come on over. The magic book of sound has a message for you. Listen, tell us what you hear, and you could be the winner of a new life!"

People turned to watch him, and Jessie laughed. She went to get a Coke for them to share. They drank some and put the cup on the ground next to them. A few moments later a couple walked by and tossed a coin into the cup. Daniel and Jessie looked up, surprised.

"What are you doing! That was our Coke!" yelled Daniel. "You think we're beggars?"

"Sorry!" replied the man, hurrying away with his wife. "You looked like—"

"Get out of here!" yelled Daniel. "Stupid people. Think before you act next time."

Embarrassed, Jessie started gathering their things together. "I think it's time to go, Daniel. It was an honest mistake. You didn't have to yell at those poor people. They were trying to be nice."

"Come on! You should be supporting me, not taking their side. I don't deserve this."

Now he's angry at me! Jessie thought. I'd better be quiet. She tried to hug Daniel, but he pulled away.

"I have to go out of town tonight," he said.

"Again?"

"Yes. Stop making me feel guilty!"

"May I ask why?"

"Are you my mother?" he replied sarcastically as he took out his phone and started making calls. Jessie backed away nervously and carried everything up to the house. She didn't understand him. One moment he was sweet and caring, and the next he was exploding. He was so unpredictable, like Dr. Jekyll and Mr. Hyde.

Daniel didn't come back to the house, so Jessie made herself dinner and opened her journal. She was hoping her journal would talk to her again, but there was nothing, so she picked up a book and read herself to sleep. The night passed slowly.

Sometime in the morning, Daniel crawled into bed. He put his hand between Jessie's legs, and she woke.

"Mmm, I love your legs . . ."

Startled, Jessie jumped up. "Good morning, my love . . . You scared me."

"I have a surprise for you."

He handed Jessie a bag with a fancy dress, a scarf, and high-heeled shoes.

"My beautiful lady, a friend of mine gave us tickets to the opera in Nice. Get dressed—we have to go soon."

He was acting as if he'd never been angry; he seemed to have forgotten all about it. Jessie put on the dress and some makeup in the bathroom while he was lying on the bed, reading the newspaper. She sashayed out like she was a model in a fashion show, and his jaw dropped.

"Oh my God, look at my gorgeous woman! You're a supermodel. I don't deserve you. I've honestly never seen a woman so beautiful."

He couldn't take his eyes off her. Jessie blushed and kissed him passionately, careful not to mess up her makeup or dress.

They walked the Promenade des Anglais, along the beach, then went to dinner and to the Opéra de Nice. Jessie had never been to an opera before. They had two of the best seats in the house, and Daniel waved and smiled at all the people he knew. The performer opened in a loud, high-pitched voice.

"Is it true that sound can break glass?" Jessie whispered in Daniel's ear.

"The right vibrations can . . . yes."

As Jessie watched the opera, she wondered why so many people loved it. It was a nice experience, but nothing she wanted to do again. She looked over at Daniel; he was asleep.

When it was over, Daniel grabbed Jessie's hand and started toward the exit, but suddenly he let go and moved in front of her. Before Jessie could say anything, a woman came over, hugged him, and gave him a kiss on each cheek.

"Daniel," she said. "It's so nice to see you."

"You, too," he said.

"How's Dorothy?"

"Oh, she's fine. Where's John?"

"He's over there with an old buddy."

Jessie stood next to him, silent. The woman looked at her and back at him, waiting to be introduced.

"This is Jessie, my colleague," said Daniel.

Jessie put on a fake smile and nodded hello. They conversed for a few minutes, and then the woman left. It was an awkward situation, and Jessie didn't like Daniel's behavior. "Why did you pull your hand away and lie to her about our relationship?" she asked.

"Come on. I didn't lie to her, I just didn't tell her the whole truth. She's Dorothy's friend."

"I thought Dorothy told you to do what you wanted."

"She did, but I also told you she doesn't want to know, and she doesn't want all her friends knowing either."

"So she gave you permission to play with other women, as long as you stay in role, and pretend to have something that you don't? What kind of relationship is that?"

There was a moment of silence.

"Do you love her?" asked Jessie.

"I love you. I've told you many times."

"Then why don't you tell her about me?"

"I just can't!"

I don't believe it, she thought. There's some other reason why he's staying married. He's using one of us, probably me.

"Jessie, you need to stop this nonsense," Daniel said. "By the way, we need to buy your ticket back to Cameroon."

"Go back? I thought you just said you loved me!"

"Your leave of absence is almost over. You told me the Peace Corps gave you just twelve weeks."

Jessie was shocked; she didn't know what to say. She clenched her jaw, and said nothing.

"Look, Jessie . . . I love you, but for now, you have to go back and take care of things. Me, too."

When they got home that night, Daniel touched Jessie intimately. Her eyes filled with tears, and she fell asleep. In the morning, Jessie didn't resist his affection, but she didn't respond as before.

"Why are you so tense?" he asked.

"I don't know."

"Really, what's bothering you?"

"Are you sure you really love me?"

"Yes, of course!"

"But would you marry me if you could?"

"Yes, I would."

"To whom are you most attached?"

"Stop being jealous; you are the woman of my life. I have nothing with Dorothy but friendship."

Jessie smiled sheepishly and looked away.

"Okay," she said. "Let's get back to the book."

"Thank you! I'd like to stop wasting time on stupid jealousies. We have a lot of work to do."

After a few deep breaths, they both regained their composure.

"So here's what we think we know about the book . . . it's written by the Word, with the divine language; it makes divine sounds, and we listen to it with our hearts," said Jessie. "All this research, and we haven't even confirmed our hypothesis."

"Right!"

"Doesn't your family have any more information about it? Surely someone knows something."

"Actually, nobody in my family knows about it. My father gave it to me secretly before he passed away last year. He told me that one day we would see in the book what no one else could."

"Wait a minute . . . that's what the angel said to Flamel in a dream. I read it on the churchyard panel in Paris."

Daniel grinned and raised his eyebrows.

"Oh my God!" said Jessie. "Is this book *that* book? Nicholas Flamel's book?"

Daniel was quiet, nodding yes.

"Your father was Nicholas Flamel?"

He shook his head, and waited.

"You are Nicholas Flamel?"

"I am a descendent of Nicholas."

"No! Why didn't you tell me before?"

"You discovered on your own."

"I don't believe this!"

"I didn't believe it either, at first."

"So it's not just a message, it's *the* message, the spiritual elixir, the path to divine and eternal life! The objective of alchemy!"

"I thought you knew this already. That's why we're studying the book, to understand."

Jessie thought about why and how they were studying the ancient book. She realized that she had been following Daniel around without thinking much about what they were really doing.

"But the Word, the divine language, is love. Love is the message of the book."

"Yes, but what we are trying to understand is the intelligence of love, which is the path to divine, eternal life, and to creation."

"But we're trying to understand with our minds, and we're supposed to understand with our hearts."

"I know, but if we want to change the world, then we have to understand with our minds."

"Daniel, that's not what you said before. . . . You said the divine language speaks to the heart, only the heart."

"My dear, we already know that the divine language speaks to the heart, to achieve harmony through love! What we are trying to discover is the intelligence behind this process, to elevate humanity and hopefully create a better world."

Jessie sighed. "This is crazy! You and I are not God! We can't just uncover the intelligence of love and re-create it, as an alchemist creates gold."

Daniel grinned. "Someday, you'll understand who I really am and who you really are, and what we are capable of doing together."

"We are two people in love with each other. We are supposed to let love move and mold us into one, but you want to be God! Lucifer wanted to be God, too, and look what happened to him. I'm afraid you're missing the whole point and purpose of the book."

"My Jessie, why do we fall in love with one person and not another? Almost everyone has been in love with someone who didn't love him back, and almost everyone has been loved by someone whom he didn't love. This is very sad. But if we can understand how it works, maybe we can create more happiness and less heartbreak."

"But—"

"The heart is getting harder and harder through the generations. If it gets too hard, we are all doomed."

Jessie didn't know how to respond. Frustrated, she went for a run. When she returned, Daniel was working in his library. He looked at her briefly, without expression, and then continued working.

Daniel wants to understand love, she thought, but I don't know if he feels love beyond the physical. There's only one way to make a man feel.

Jessie walked over, put her arms around his neck, and kissed Daniel passionately. At first he turned his head and tried to resist her. Then he picked her up and carried her to bed. They made love for hours.

"Are you okay?" asked Daniel. "You look a little sad."

"I'm fine, my love."

They both stared at each other thoughtfully.

"Listen, I would like to start over with our discussion. I don't think we can read this book in the way we are trying to," said Jessie.

"Okay, what do you suggest?"

"I don't know, but while I was running, I was thinking. What's in that book is inside us. We were created, and we create; so we are both the sand and the sound."

Daniel jumped up.

"Of course! Why didn't I think of it before?"

"What?" asked Jessie.

"We need to put the sand on the pages."

"I thought you said you already tried that?"

"I never used the pages for the sand; I used the pages to make the sound. But the book makes its own sound."

"Do you mean the sound that we cannot hear?"

"Yes, it's always sounding. We don't read the sound that *we* make with the metal pages; we can't! We read the sand, forming in response to the *eternal* sound."

"I see what you mean. Okay, let's go try it out," said Jessie. "Maybe you're right."

The two of them went to a secluded area of the beach with no wind. Daniel cleared a flat spot and laid down a cloth. Then he placed the metal pages side by side and sprinkled sand on them.

Suddenly the sand started to tremble and take form.

"Holy cow!" yelled Jessie.

Daniel put his hand over her mouth. "Don't interfere with the vibrations, please," he whispered in her ear.

They quietly watched it form into what looked like ancient symbols, one on each page. Finally the sand stopped shifting.

"What language is that?" asked Jessie. "Do you know?"

"No. I've never seen it before."

12
Illusions

Stacks of papers collapsed, and a book slid off, crashing onto the floor. Jessie and Daniel were going through Daniel's library, looking for information that could help them uncover the meaning of the symbols.

"Daniel, I've never seen so many old manuscripts in such a mess. You really need to take better care of what you have."

Daniel smirked.

"What's this?" she asked, uncurling a roll of parchment, stained and torn around the edges. Aleph and Bet, the first two symbols of the Hebrew alphabet, were elegantly handpainted on it in brilliant red and royal blue. Gold laced through and around, joining them like lovers.

Daniel leaned over to see. "One of my favorite medieval pieces. I found this beauty at the antique market not long ago."

Jessie knew that each Hebrew letter carried its own profound meaning, associated with a number; Aleph was one, and Bet was two. Naturally, she was drawn to Bet. It was more open than Aleph, holding the whole concept of duality in its form: two realms, physical and spiritual; two Torahs, written and oral; two forces, thought and feeling; and two genders, male and female. As Eve came from Adam, Bet came from Aleph, carrying both in its nature.

"Ancient letters are infused with so much meaning, and we don't even know it," said Jessie. "That the sound of a spoken letter can move sand into the shape of its written symbol is beyond all comprehension."

"It proves there's an intelligent force in the universe. I've always been fascinated with the Aleph-Bet relationship. It's sacred. Everything, all language, grew from these two letters intermeshing with each other."

The letters were in love, Jessie thought. That's what the artist was saying.

They continued going through the disorganized library with a keen eye on ancient symbols and languages. "I hope we find something soon," said Jessie. "I'm tired."

At that moment Daniel's phone rang. He took the call in the other room. Jessie couldn't hear well, but his voice was low, warm, and affectionate. About five minutes later he came back in the library.

"Who was that?" asked Jessie.

"My wife."

"I heard you call her your love."

"Come on. We're married. I think it's normal."

Jessie was quiet. Maybe I'm just a tool, she thought. Maybe he just misses affection, since his wife can't have relations with him.

"Don't be jealous," said Daniel. "You are my love. By the way, what time is your flight on Monday?"

"In the morning . . . Why do you ask?"

"I just want to make sure I'm back in time to take you to the airport."

"You're leaving again?"

"Jessie, I wish I could stay, but I can't."

"What could be more important than being together in my final days here? Where are you going?"

"My wife needs me to take her to a clinic in Paris. There's nobody else to take her."

"Have they found out what she has yet?"

"They don't know exactly."

In the evening, Jessie was again alone with her journal.

What happened? Why did you stop communicating with me? Is Daniel being honest? I am very nervous.

She went away and came back. There was no response, so she wrote more.

Daniel is hiding something. I want the truth. Please, I beg you to talk to me again. I told you I'm sorry if I pushed you away. I didn't mean to get angry.

Daniel was gone for several days, leaving Jessie alone, walking by the sea and reading books. She e-mailed him several times to express her love, but he only replied once: "Thank you, my dear."

Full of mistrust and fear, she picked up the ancient book and shook it. Then she put it on the bed and kneeled over it, crying. "I don't trust Daniel anymore," she told the book. "He's too mysterious. Please speak—to my journal, to my heart, to my mind. Say something!"

After a good cry, Jessie searched Daniel's drawers for anything that might help her understand. She stumbled upon a file with passwords, including the password to his e-mail. She wrote it in her journal, just in case she might need it later on.

For the next few days, she stayed in the house alone. It wasn't as enchanting as it had seemed before; her perspective had changed. She was too lonely, thinking too much, confused in her mind.

Daniel returned very tired the night before Jessie's departure. He went straight to the bedroom, put his pajamas on, and lay down with the newspaper. Then he told Jessie to come closer, so he could hug her.

"How was your trip?" she asked.

"Fine. I think this doctor may be able to help her. It wasn't easy to get an appointment with him, but I have connections."

"Did he figure out what she has?"

"No, but he's trying."

Without getting up, Daniel lifted his head and looked around the room. "Have you seen my phone?" he asked. "Oh, jeez, I think I left it in the car."

"Don't worry. I'll go get it. Just relax."

Jessie put on a jacket and went down the steps to the car. After shuffling through all the papers and trash on his seat, she found it and started back up to the house. Just then a message popped up on the phone. It was from Daniel's wife.

Thank you for the wonderful time in Paris, my love. You're the best husband in the world. Are you going to get that painting we liked at the auction?

Something inside Jessie started to burn, anger mixed with despair. *He lied to me. She's not sick. He took her for pleasure.*

When Jessie returned to the room, Daniel was sleeping. She put his phone on the night table and got into bed. Unable to rest, she watched him sleep and tried to read his face. In the early morning, he tried to make love with her, but she pretended that she was in deep sleep. She didn't want him to even touch her.

On the way to the airport, they were both quiet. After Jessie checked in, Daniel received a phone call and put the caller on hold. Then he bear-hugged Jessie and kissed her passionately.

"I'm sorry, but I have to run," he said.

Jessie nodded as if she understood and made her way to the gate. Once she was on the plane, she thought about Daniel and started to cry. The problem was, she loved him and she knew it. She couldn't stop. The whole trip she made herself miserable, wondering if Daniel really loved her or if it was all a bad joke. She went over every detail of their relationship, looking for clues.

In Yaoundé, she took a taxi to the Peace Corps Center and went straight to the director. He looked surprised and confused to see her.

"Don't you remember? I called you before I left, and you approved a family medical leave for me. You were going to investigate while I was gone," she said, perplexed.

"Oh, yes, you received a threatening letter under your door. Let me check on that. You can stay next door in the volunteer house. Come back after tomorrow, and I should have more information."

Jessie went next door. The main room was full of beds with backpacks on them. All the volunteers passing through stayed there; it was a refuge, but without privacy. She found an empty bed and claimed it. Then she found a computer to e-mail Daniel:

Subject: I made it
From: jessielynnfreedman@gmail.com
To: daniel.lumiel@orange.fr

Dear Daniel,

I just wanted to let you know that I made it back to
Cameroon safely. They still don't know what they are
going to do with me, but I should hear soon. I don't
want to go back to my village. I don't belong there.
Honestly, I don't know where I belong anymore. It's
hot here. I miss you.

Love,
Jessie

She needed to talk to someone, but she didn't know who.
Then she remembered that Amina's stepfather lived in Yaoundé,
and she could call. To her surprise, Amina was there visiting her
stepfather since her new husband was out of town. Surprised
and excited, Amina gave Jessie directions. It was about thirty
minutes' walk down the street, through a market, and up a hill.

When Jessie arrived, Amina jumped up from the couch
and hugged her. Then she broke into tears. Although she had
just married, her husband was already courting another woman
and planning to take her as his wife. That's why he was out of
town. He was visiting the other woman's family and making
arrangements.

"He told me he wasn't going to marry anyone else."

"Men cannot be trusted," said Jessie.

"If I had only known."

After listening for a while and trying to sympathize with

Amina, Jessie started to tell her about all the strange things that had happened in her village, and how she had gone to find Daniel. Just then Amina's stepfather walked in.

"Excuse me, Amina, your sisters need you now," he said. "Jessie, I'm so glad you could visit. I hope that you're staying for dinner."

Amina left, and Jessie found herself alone with the stepfather. He smiled at her and sat down on the bed. She didn't know what it was, but something about him made her uncomfortable.

"Amina talks about you all the time," he said. "It's true . . . you are very pretty. So, what brings you to Yaoundé?"

"I have some business with the Peace Corps," Jessie said. "If you'll excuse me, I think I'll go help Amina."

Jessie got up quickly and left the room. The daughters were in the kitchen, serving food on plates. Jessie picked one up with each hand and started walking to the dining room, but one of the girls stopped her.

"No!" she said. "*We* serve the food. You are the guest. Please go to the dining room and sit with our father and brothers at the table."

Jessie looked at Amina. "Please, I want to eat with you, not them. I don't feel comfortable—"

"No, Jessie. Go to the table. I will find you afterward."

Reluctantly, Jessie ate at the table with the men. She was quiet, keeping her mouth full of food and eating quickly. They asked her questions, and she just nodded yes or no. As soon as she'd eaten, she thanked them, excused herself, and went to find Amina.

"That was fast!" said Amina.

"I wasn't very hungry."

"You? Not hungry?"

"Listen, Amina, I'm having trouble, and I need some advice."

"My grandmother is very good at helping people. Actually, she is my stepfather's mother. She sees things that others don't."

While this wasn't the reply that Jessie had been expecting, she followed Amina to visit this grandmother in the house next door. The woman was old and couldn't stand. They sat down next to her in a chair, and Amina spoke in Fulfulde.

The woman grabbed Jessie's hand and turned it over, looking at the lines in her palm. She looked at the other hand, too, and put them together. Then she looked over Jessie's face and eyes, and touched her cheek softly. Her hands smelled like orange peels.

"What's she doing?" asked Jessie.

"She's reading you," replied Amina.

After a moment of silence, the grandmother spoke in her African tongue for what seemed like a long time.

"My grandmother said you are an extraordinary young woman. There's something different about you, but she doesn't know what it is. She can't see you any older, which means you're going to die young. She thinks she saw someone chasing you. He was dark."

A chill ran down Jessie's spine. "Did she know about the tarantula diviner? Did you ever tell her what he said?" she asked.

"No, I didn't even tell her who you are."

Jessie waited quietly while Amina finished talking with her grandmother, mulling it over in her mind. Who could be chasing her? How was she going to die? They went back to Amina's room. Jessie was nervous, desperate to talk.

"So I stayed with Daniel for three months in France," said Jessie. "I've never felt so in love."

Amina listened for a while, but then broke in. "It sounds like Daniel really helped you, but I wonder who is this dark figure chasing you."

"I don't know. This may sound strange, but sometimes it feels like Daniel."

"Wait a minute—you just told me that Daniel saved you, and now you're telling me that he may be the one chasing you? Do you know how ridiculous that sounds?"

"I don't know . . . it's just a feeling. I'm confused."

"What about?"

"I just don't know if I can trust him. I didn't tell you, but he's married, and he doesn't want to leave his wife."

"Oh, come on. He isn't chasing you. Think about it—do you even want to marry him?"

"Of course," replied Jessie. "I don't have to think about it. I know he's the one for me."

"Then you'd be his wife, and he could do the same thing to you that he's doing to his wife now, and my husband is doing to me."

"Good point. I hadn't thought of it that way."

"It doesn't matter that men can't take other wives in your culture. They still take what they need. Be thankful you're the one he really needs!"

"You're right. Maybe it's better not to get married."

"Just remember, you could be in my shoes."

"I'm sorry, Amina. I know how you must feel."

It was too late to go back to the volunteer house, so Amina told Jessie to stay the night. They lay down together in a small twin-size bed. There was no other choice; all the other beds were taken. Jessie didn't sleep well; she couldn't move.

In the early morning, she returned to the Peace Corps Center and checked her e-mail. There were no messages from Daniel. She wondered why he didn't write her back and what he was doing.

Spontaneously, she took out her journal and turned to where she'd written down the URL and password for his e-mail. After hastily considering the consequences, she logged in. He had lots of messages, several from a woman named Jacqueline. Curious, Jessie opened one.

Subject: Re: Finally
From: jjaltier@orange.fr
To: daniel.lumiel@orange.fr

Good night, my love. I'm so happy to see you soon.
Big kiss.

Subject: Re: Finally
From: daniel.lumiel@orange.fr
To: jjaltier@orange.fr

Good night, my darling and accomplice.

-----Original Message-----

Subject: Finally
From: jjaltier@orange.fr
To: daniel.lumiel@orange.fr

It seems that your soul mate, your love, will meet you in
Venice. Alone we are weak, but together we are strong.
Lots of kisses.

Soul mate? Jessie gripped her stomach in pain. She noticed
another woman's name, Joanne, on several messages.

Subject: Re: Hugs
From: daniel.lumiel@orange.fr
To: joanne1974@yahoo.com

Why is it that every time I try to hug you, my arms come back to my chest? When will you come?

Subject: Re: Hugs
From: joanne1974@yahoo.com
To: daniel.lumiel@orange.fr

I agree. But for now I send you my soul in the wind and a poem from my heart.

Subject: Re: Hugs
From: daniel.lumiel@orange.fr
To: joanne1974@yahoo.com

Giovannissima. How are you, my love? The day will be beautiful when I can see you again.

-----Original Message-----

Subject: Hugs
From: joanne1974@yahoo.com
To: daniel.lumiel@orange.fr

It's a beautiful day . . . I am sending you a big hug in the wind.

Tears came to Jessie's eyes. She covered her face with her hands and started sobbing. Embarrassed that other people might see her, she got up and started walking to the bathroom. A woman was coming up the stairs.

"Anna!" Jessie said, covering her eyes.

"Hi, Jessie! Are you okay? What's going on?"

Jessie searched her mind for something to share with Anna that wasn't the whole truth.

"I'm having some problems in my village. Someone is threatening me, perhaps chasing me."

"Do you know who it is?"

"No, I don't."

"That's too bad. Well, I hope they catch him."

"Me, too. I'm not feeling well. Excuse me."

Jessie went to the bathroom, locked the door, and fell to her knees. *Lies. All lies.* When she'd regained her composure, she went to bed and pretended to be sick all day and most of the night. She took some pills to help her sleep, but she had nightmares. Her sensei's shadow had returned to taunt her. Or had it been there lurking all along?

Before dawn, while the other volunteers were sleeping, Jessie got up and went back to the computer. There was a lump in her throat, and she swallowed hard.

"You're up early."

Jessie jumped up, startled by the voice.

"Oh, Anna, you scared me."

"Sorry, I guess you didn't hear me when I walked in. I have an early train to catch, but are you sure you're okay?"

"Yes, Anna. Thanks for your concern. Have a safe trip, and keep in touch."

"Okay, Jessie. If you need anything, let me know."

Jessie was alone again, staring at the computer. She tried to write Daniel, but the words wouldn't come out right, and she kept deleting and starting over. This went on for hours.

At eight o'clock, she went to the Peace Corps Center to see if they had made any decisions. The office was supposed to be open, but the door was locked. To calm her nerves, she went for a walk around the block. When she returned, it was open, and the director had arrived.

"It's not safe for you to go back to your village," he said. "And there are no vacant positions in Cameroon. So you have two options. You can either resign and go back to the United States, or you can take a position that we found for you in Ecuador."

"That's in Latin America, right?"

"In the northeast part of South America, south of Colombia. You'd have to leave tomorrow; training starts in three days."

Jessie couldn't go back to Daniel now, and she didn't want to go back to the States, so she agreed to go to Ecuador. Before packing, she found herself at the computer once again, this time to check her own e-mail. Seconds after she logged in, a message arrived from Daniel.

Subject: My Beautiful Lady
From: daniel.lumiel@orange.fr
To: jessielynnfreedman@gmail.com

Hi Jessie,

What's going on with the Peace Corps? I super love you and miss you.

Daniel

All Jessie could see were lies. Not wanting to love him, she prayed silently for the feeling to go away. She tried to cover her emotions, writing only a few words back.

Subject: Re: My Beautiful Lady
From: jessielynnfreedman@gmail.com
To: daniel.lumiel@orange.fr

No time to write now. They are moving me to Ecuador, and I have to get ready.

13
To the Bridge

Flying into Quito was like a dream, with big fluffy clouds, green mountains, and snowcapped volcanoes. The wheels hit the ground hard, and the plane wobbled from side to side as the pilot slammed on the brakes.

With a Peace Corps driver in a big van, Jessie and a pack of new trainees got their first glimpse of the city. It was more congested than she had imagined, and the pollution was awful. As they edged through it slowly, as if they were stuck in the mud, a big puff of black smoke burst out of a bus beside them and into the window.

Jessie could feel her skin caked with soot. It took them about an hour to get out of traffic and down to the valley of Tumbaco, where the training center was. She was happy to be out of the city, where she could breathe fresh, clean air. It was slightly cool and crisp, and the sunshine felt good.

As before, the trainees were assigned host families and sent off with them. Jessie's host mother was a short indigenous woman with long black hair. She was much older than Iya was and uninterested in befriending young Americans. She hosted many trainees for supplemental income; for her, it was nothing but business.

A few days passed, and Jessie settled back in to her busy routine as a trainee. It felt strange to be back in the rhythm of school. In the morning she went to Spanish class, and in the afternoon she went to technical training. No matter how hard she tried to focus on her new life, though, she couldn't stop thinking about Daniel.

I ran away from my sensei. I stopped loving him after he abused me. So why can't I stop loving Daniel? He is just going to use and hurt me.

Several days into training, Jessie's stomach continued to feel nervous, and her back hurt all the time. She went to see a doctor at the Peace Corps Center. He examined her thoroughly and asked several questions.

"You need to relax," he said. "Your back is very tense because you're full of stress. What's going on?"

"Moving to another country and starting over with everything is not easy."

"Well, whatever it is, I'm giving you a relaxant and a pain reliever. Take one of each every four hours. Do you think you need an antidepressant too?"

"No, thank you. I don't like to take too many medications. I have some herbal teas that help."

She longed for something to take away her love for Daniel, like the witch doctor who'd broken Albert's spell. Maybe a good shaman could help her. Ecuador was known for its legendary shamans.

At the end of her first week, Jessie and her class piled into an old yellow school bus for a field trip. She stared out the window as they wound through the mountains along the edge of steep cliffs. There were no guardrails; if the driver were to go too far off the road, they would all die.

In almost two hours they arrived in Otavalo, a popular weaving community near the equator. All the trainees got out and stretched. After a big lunch in a small café, they went to the market. There were tapestries, felt hats, and ponchos everywhere. The other trainees were eager to shop, but Jessie didn't feel like being a typical tourist, and wandered around aimlessly.

"Miss, tell me what you like . . . good price," said a lady behind one of the vending tables who was selling all kinds of sweaters.

Jessie smiled and shook her head.

"Are you in pain?" the lady asked.

"Pardon me?"

"The way you're standing, it looks like you're in pain."

Suddenly conscious of her hunched posture, Jessie pulled herself up straight and tried to hold the position.

"My husband is one of the best shamans around. People from everywhere come to see him."

Jessie raised one eyebrow. Could this be the shaman she'd been waiting for? If he couldn't take away her love for Daniel, he might at least make her feel better.

After telling her group leader that she would be back soon, she went with the woman to her dark, modest house. A short older man with greasy salt-and-pepper hair looked up. His eyes were red and glassy, as if he'd been smoking marijuana.

There was a shamanic certification on the wall. The man didn't ask any questions; he just gave Jessie a candle and told her to rub it all over her body. When she had finished, he lit the candle with his cigarette. Then he blew smoke over it a few times until it started to drip wax.

He told Jessie to remove her clothing down to her underwear and bra. Uneasy and embarrassed, she looked to the shaman's wife for permission. When the woman nodded, Jessie removed her pants and shirt.

With a serious expression, the shaman took a swig of moonshine, swished it around, and spewed it all over Jessie's body. Completely unprepared, Jessie cringed. What had she gotten herself into? She willed herself to relax as he spat the liquor at her again and again until she was drenched with moonshine; it would soon be over.

Finally he dried her off with the fur of a live guinea pig. As soon as he'd finished, without warning, he began to cough, hacking violently. Jessie frantically turned toward his wife again, but she just smiled and nodded, as if everything was happening the way it should.

Next, the shaman rolled an egg over Jessie's entire body. When he passed it between her legs, she felt very uncomfortable, but she remained calm, praying silently that soon it would all be over.

When he stopped for a moment, she thought he was done, but he was just fetching a bunch of weedy-looking plant stems. He whipped her all over with the prickly, stinging leaves, giving her a rash and hives. Then he held the lighted candle in front of him and spewed moonshine at it so that flames licked at her body. Jessie prayed silently, terrified that her hair would catch fire.

When it was finally over, she stood frozen for a moment, fearful that some new shock was coming. The shaman's wife told her to get dressed, but she could only move very slowly. She felt weak, a little dizzy, strange, but calm and peaceful. Her back pain was gone.

The man left the room, and the two women walked back to the market together.

"Do you feel better?" the shaman's wife asked.

"Yes, much better. I don't know how he did it without massaging or manipulating anything."

"He helped you come into the right relationship with Mother Earth and all her inhabitants."

"How does it work? I don't understand."

"Sacred communication with the spirit world. You cannot understand unless you become a shaman."

As they approached the market, someone waved to Jessie: it was time to go. Jessie thanked the woman and picked up the pace. The bus pulled out as soon as she got on, and she relaxed into her seat. It was true that she felt freer, more balanced, connected to something bigger than herself.

On the way back, they stopped by Mitad del Mundo, where tourists visit the equator. A painted orange line marked the boundary between the northern and southern hemispheres, and the trainees took pictures of each other straddling it, standing on both sides of the world.

Afterward they went to Pululahua, a dormant volcano nearby, and to a museum there. If they tried to walk on the lines painted in the museum, their guide said, they would feel strong magnetic forces pushing them over. Curious, Jessie closed her eyes and started to walk along one of the lines. She couldn't take a single step without falling to one side; indeed, something seemed to be pushing her over.

After she'd tried many times to walk the line, without success, the guide gave Jessie a piece of black jade and asked her to walk the line again. "The sacred stone from the volcano gives us strength and balance," she explained. Jessie was amazed; she could now walk along the line without falling over. What did a stone have to do with her balance?

"I don't understand how this is working," she said.

"Everything is alive, interacting with its surroundings," said the guide.

"Stones are alive?"

"To exist is to be alive; spirit is the source."

She remembered the stone at Iya's house and the witch doctor who'd cast out the evil spirit. It wasn't the same idea, though it was close. In Iya's world there were evil spirits, but in this world there was only harmony and discord.

On the bus, Jessie opened her backpack and took out her journal.

The shaman is a kind of alchemist, but more collective and spiritual, communicating with the spirit world daily. To the shaman, harmony is a way, not a destination, and one does not achieve it through love. This means that love is something bigger than harmony, and beyond. Maybe it starts as a seed in our hearts. Maybe we make it grow by following our hearts. And maybe it moves us through a master plan of the Word. Perhaps this is what is happening to me with Daniel.

When the bus returned to the training center, it was just after five o'clock. Jessie raced inside to find a computer. If her love was all part of the plan, then maybe she had misinterpreted what was going on with Daniel. Could it be that he did love her, and he was faithful, but his life was just complicated? Had she jumped to conclusions? She decided to check Daniel's e-mail once again, hoping to understand. But there she found another conversation with yet another woman, Barbara.

Subject: Re: When you return
From: daniel.lumiel@orange.fr

To: barbara3567@yahoo.com

Ooh la la.

Subject: Re: When you return
From: barbara3567@yahoo.com
To: daniel.lumiel@orange.fr

I miss you. When you come back, chocolate and unbridled sex.

-----Original Message-----

Subject: When you return
From: daniel.lumiel@orange.fr
To: barbara3567@yahoo.com

Go to the window for kisses over your whole body. Do you hear them tapping on the glass?

Jessie's back and shoulder muscles tightened. She felt that awful sensation in her stomach again. She leaned back, trying to inhale. It felt as if she couldn't breathe. Anguished and confused, she found a phone and dialed. It rang several times with no answer. She tried again.

"Hello," he answered, his voice cracking.

"It's Jessie. . . . Were you sleeping?"

"It's midnight here . . . yes! How are you, my love? Is something wrong?"

"Yes, I'm not feeling well," she cried.

"What's wrong?"

"You! You lied to me! You didn't take your wife to Paris to see a doctor, you took her for fun."

"What are you talking about?"

"I saw her message pop up when I went to get your phone that you left in the car."

"Wait a minute. I took you around in Paris too, and you had a nice time. Be fair!"

"Fair? What does being fair have to do with your lying and sneaking around?"

"We went to the doctor like I told you, but we did other things, too. If Dorothy wants me to take her to Paris for a weekend, then I need to take her. Finished!"

"She thinks you're the best husband in the world! Bah! If she only knew. How many women are there? How many women does one man need?"

"Just you! I have not kissed, touched, or done anything with any other woman since I met you. What are you talking about?"

"Oh, really?"

"Yes, really!"

"Barbara? Joanne? Jacqueline?"

There were several seconds of silence.

"You are spying on me?" Daniel said finally. "I never told you anything about them."

"That's right—you don't tell me anything, so how else am I supposed to find the truth? I needed to know more. So tell me what is going on, please."

Daniel chuckled awkwardly. "Those ladies that you refer to are just friends! They're old ladies . . . and they're ugly. You insult me even thinking that I could be involved with any of them."

"Oh, okay. So if I was not young and beautiful, then you wouldn't be interested in me either, right?"

"Come on, Jessie. You got it all wrong!"

"And you expect me to believe, after reading your correspondence, that you are just being 'friendly' with these women? Seriously?"

"Yes! We were just playing with words, that's all."

"You must think I'm stupid."

Daniel sighed. "Jessie, we have to face the facts. I'm sorry, but our relationship isn't working."

Jessie's heart sank. Her eyes filled with tears.

"Just like that? You end our love without even an explanation? It's bad enough you lied! Now you kill me with your love! For what? For pride?"

"You don't trust me! And what you did is terrible. I would never have invaded your privacy. I'm sorry, but I don't feel peace with you anymore. I can't trust you!"

"You're pathetic. It's you who destroyed our peace, not me. You, with your women!"

Daniel laughed. "My women?" he replied. "I told you, I was joking around with friends . . . that's all."

"Still, you think it's appropriate to joke flirtatiously with other women?"

"I wasn't flirting! I did nothing wrong!"

"Okay, so I can do the same with other men, if they are old and ugly, of course . . . and if I'm just joking."

"Go do what you want! You were the one, but it's over. We're finished! I don't want anything to do with you."

"No, I don't accept this! You said you loved me, and that we were going to change the world together."

"I need peace. I'm sorry, but this is too much. Don't contact me again. If you try, I will not answer." There was a click, and then only a buzz over the line.

Jessie ran out into the pouring rain, as fast as her legs would go. Headlights bounced off a stream of water rushing down the street. Tires screeched as she dashed across the road and disappeared into the bush.

Rain poured, and thunder cracked. The sun had almost set. She remembered her father talking to his family about the divorce. Her mother and brother were listening; she was crying.

She moved through the humid, heavy air, breathing deeply. Lightning illuminated an obscure place in her mind. There was her sensei, slithering into her body. She saw him watching her. He looked like Daniel.

Water gushed from her shoes as she pounded the ground. The path was narrowing and the vegetation getting thicker. Suddenly the rain stopped, and Jessie with it. There was only silence, and darkness.

Then there was light.

Her heart was racing; she gasped for breath. A full moon broke through the clouds, and she could see the dirt path ahead, winding through the trees. To her right, a weathered wooden bridge, its missing planks giving it a snaggletoothed look, its handrails broken in places, stretched over a deep ravine with a rocky creek at the bottom.

Jessie gripped the rails and started to cross. There was no one in sight. A board came loose and fell; it felt like a long time before she heard it strike the rocks below. The bridge wobbled frighteningly, but she kept moving toward the center. She released her grip and raised her hands to the sky. The moon shone in her eyes, and she closed them.

Rainwater mixed with sweat dripped down her face, into her mouth, as she screamed at the top of her lungs. "You tease me with love! You let them rape and mutilate my soul! Some god you are. Well, I'm not playing your cruel games anymore."

Jessie released her mind from life and leaned forward.

A gust of wind whipped past her ears, then a voice.

"Jessie, Jessie . . ."

Jessie caught her balance and opened her eyes. She looked around; nobody. What was going on?

"Jessie, Jessie, Jessie . . ." came the voice again.

"Where are you?"

"I'm right here."

"How do you know my name?"

"Because we have the same name."

Jessie was quiet, paralyzed. She didn't know what to think or how to react.

"If you do this, you will kill me."

"How?"

"You will take away my body."

"Okay, who are you?" she said sternly, full of fear.

"One who understands you and what you seek."

Her mind flashed back to Daniel on the giant pile of cotton; those were *his* words, but this wasn't his voice.

"Okay, no more games. Show me you are real."

There was a long pause, and just when Jessie thought it was all a figment of her imagination, the voice spoke again.

"Your father left you. Your sensei took advantage of you. Now you think Daniel is using you. You've had a hard life, and you don't trust anyone."

Jessie was quiet, trembling. Clouds blocked the light of the moon, and the bridge was dark.

"Everybody is *looking* for love. They are trying to find it in someone else. This is why the world is such a mess."

"Love doesn't exist," Jessie replied. "It's just a fantasy we create, in our search for purpose in this ridiculous life and world."

"Is that why you wanted to jump off this bridge? Because

you stopped believing in love? And you think your life is for nothing?"

"That's right. Daniel was my last hope. I trusted him, and he betrayed me."

"Good. Now that you've stopped believing, you can start creating this love that you desire."

"Come on, that's ridiculous. I have created it. I love Daniel. It's not me with the problem."

"You said before that love doesn't exist, and now you're saying it does exist inside you. Does it or doesn't it exist?"

"Who are you?" asked Jessie.

"I am the source of creation."

Jessie thought for a moment. "The creation of what? Good or evil?"

"There is no creation of evil. Evil is a cancer in what is created, to *de-create* and destroy."

"You are the voice from my journal! You are the Word, aren't you?"

"I am the Word," said the voice. "But you are my body. This is why you must create love."

"Out of what? Nothing? Even the alchemist uses metal to make gold!"

"You have everything you need to create love, and you've already started. But now you're hindering yourself."

"So I'm supposed to take my fear, anger, and pain and miraculously transform it into love? And would you like me to die on the cross, too?"

"Stop being sarcastic and listen. I am speaking and moving through your heart. The first step is harmony within yourself."

The wind moved the clouds, and the moon lit up everything around her. For a moment Jessie felt the harmony. It was the way, the path, not the destination, just as she had written in her journal.

"I understand it's through harmony that I create love, but I don't know how to get there, and stay," she said.

"You have to give yourself freely, exactly as your heart directs, without blocking yourself in the process. This will make your love grow. Can you do this?"

"I'll try, but how can I be sure it's my heart directing me, and not something else in my mind? I don't understand the language of the heart. There's too much confusion in my mind."

"Tune your heart the same way you tune your ears, and you will know how to follow."

"But how? Please explain."

There was no answer. She waited, then asked again, but the voice was gone. Jessie took a deep breath and looked around to make sure she was still alive. Some small creature scurried along the rail. The chorus of insects roared. She flicked a bug off her leg and slowly started off the bridge. She felt lighter, freer. She felt ready to try.

14
Christopher

After a good night's sleep, Jessie attempted to send an e-mail to Daniel, but it bounced back undelivered. She tried to call him, but her number appeared to be blocked. So she wrote him a letter and put it in the mail.

Dear Daniel,

I am writing to apologize for invading your privacy and jumping to conclusions about what I saw in your messages. I didn't trust you because I was afraid to lose myself. There's only one problem with this kind of fear: to lose you is to lose myself and help no one.

I know that you don't want to continue a romantic relationship with me, but if you are serious about uncovering the intelligence of love, then we should keep working together. I had an amazing experience with the Word, and I can tell you the world desperately needs love. I have a vague idea of how to get there.

Have you found the meaning of the symbols in the book?
I'm anxious to discover.
I hope to hear from you soon.

Jessie

In the afternoon Jessie went to the Peace Corps library. As she browsed through the books, one about letting go of the past caught her eye. She picked it up and opened it. After turning a few pages, she put it back on the shelf. Nobody could help her let go, she thought; she could only find harmony within herself.

She had just sat down at a table when a young man walked in. He sat across from her and opened what looked like his journal. She couldn't help but notice him, as he began to write. He had short dark brown hair and brown eyes. His height was the same as Jessie's, and his build was muscular. He was wearing thick glasses, a button-down white shirt, jeans, and flat sneakers.

After about ten minutes, the young man stopped writing and looked at Jessie, who was focused now on her own words, penning them in her journal.

I was wrong to say I don't know what love is, because I feel it for Daniel. My heart is telling me to give to him and think about him affectionately, and my mind is telling me that he doesn't deserve my love because he is not honest and trustworthy. The result is a storm of conflict and pain.

"We have something in common," said the man.

Jessie looked up. He glanced at his journal and pen to show her what he meant.

"It appears so," said Jessie.

"You look really serious."

Jessie put her pen down and laughed. "Because I'm writing deep things."

"Sorry. Please don't let me stop you."

"It's okay, I'm getting too deep anyway."

"May I ask about what? Or is it too personal?"

"Big conflict between my heart and mind."

"If it helps, the French philosopher Blaise Pascal said, 'The heart has reasons that reason cannot know.' People who follow their hearts are happier."

Jessie was surprised by his intelligent response. She was expecting something lighter and more casual from such a young-looking man. She decided to test him more, by going deeper.

"The problem is, I've followed my heart, and it took me to some pretty painful and scary places. Now my mind is slamming on the brakes, and my heart is running full force."

He nodded as if he understood exactly what Jessie was going through. "Be careful with your mind, it's stopping your heart. This is the beginning of illness, particularly autoimmune disease and cancer."

"Wow! Those are wise words," replied Jessie. "How'd you get so smart?"

"I double majored in philosophy and religion. And my mother died from cancer, so I know a lot about that, too."

"I'm so sorry."

"Just don't make the same mistake she did. She was so angry with my father. He deserved it, but she did not."

"Nobody thinks right when they're angry," Jessie agreed.

"And anger really only hurts the self." The young man looked at his watch. "Yikes, I have to go. Maybe I'll catch you later, and we can talk more."

"What's your name anyway?"

"Christopher. And yours?"

"I'm Jessie. Nice to meet you."

When he left, Jessie went back to her journal.

I need to stop the conflict between my mind and heart. What my mind really wants is for Daniel to love me as I love him, or at least as I expect a man to love his woman. My heart wants to love him freely.

The next day, Jessie was in Spanish class looking out the window when Christopher surprised her by walking into the room. When he saw her, he stumbled backward jokingly, pretending to be awestruck. "It's you again," he said, smiling at Jessie, then announced to the room, "I'm here for the afternoon field trip."

The instructor nodded, and Christopher introduced himself to the class before sitting down in the only vacant seat, next to Jessie, propping an ankle on his knee and his chin on his hand. Jessie giggled to herself; he looked like Christopher Reeves as Clark Kent.

The instructor finished his lesson and motioned for everyone to get up. Christopher smiled and led the way to the bus. They were going to Quito, about twenty minutes away, where he lived and worked as a Peace Corps Volunteer.

Quito was the highest capital in the world, he explained, with an elevation of 9,350 feet. He would show them the highlights, but they wouldn't be able to see everything in a city of two million people.

They went to a museum, walked down the popular street of Amanonas, and took a cable car to the Cruz Loma lookout.

Jessie was by herself, gazing at snowcapped volcanoes against the green mountains, when Christopher approached.

"I've been here so many times, and I never get tired of the views," he said.

"Me neither," said Jessie. "I'm in complete awe."

"And to think about where it all came from, and how it came to be, is mind-boggling."

Jessie looked at him with surprise.

"For someone who supposedly follows his heart, you really do think too much, like me," she said.

"From atoms to solar systems, the one verse—the 'uni' verse—is moving outward in perfect balance. Is that what forms eternity?"

Jessie wondered about this peculiar young man. He was too intellectual to be real. Could it be that he was somehow, in some way, sent by the Word? "You impress me with your deep nature," she said.

"Good!" said Christopher. "Most people just think I'm weird. I've always been a loner."

Jessie laughed. "People think I'm weird too. They don't say it, but I know."

At the end of the day Jessie went home and fell into bed. She remembered standing on the bridge, and the voice calling her to create love. It told her she had already started, that she was hindering herself. Had she really started? If so, what was disrupting the process? Taking a deep breath with her whole being, she picked up her journal.

Dear Mind,

Ceasefire! Here's why you must listen to our heart now, and vow to work together. It's the only way we will succeed in this journey of life.

1. It is part of the plan to love Daniel.
2. It's for something bigger than ourselves.
3. Harmony is our first step in this process.
4. Without heart is without harmony.
5. Without harmony, we cannot go on.

I hope that you seriously consider this request to cooperate with the heart. The heart is not our enemy. You must let us love, and help us love. It is our destiny.

Jessie

In the morning Jessie went to class feeling freer. She thought about Daniel fondly again, remembering all the good things about him. She realized that if it weren't for him, she wouldn't be here today. Her purpose was not in how he felt about her, but in what she felt for him.

As she continued to dwell on his goodness, a powerful feeling rose inside her. Everything was clear; she was not distracted as she had been before. She accepted this moment, this place, these people, as part of her. She was supposed to love Daniel for some reason greater than herself, and that was that.

When class was over, the other trainees darted out the door while Jessie gathered her things casually. Her Spanish instructor patted her on the back and smiled. "Nice job today, Jessie. You did very well."

"Thanks—see you tomorrow."

Christopher was waiting outside.

"You again?" she said, jokingly.

"I wanted to see if you'd like to get some lunch."

"Sure, let's go."

Christopher took her to a small family place with organic food about ten minutes from the training center. They both sat outside and ordered the special: lentils with rice, salad, and juice. The waiter brought their juice first, and Jessie guzzled it down.

"I love this tree tomato. I never had it before coming here. There are such delicious fruits in Ecuador."

"Because of its unique position and all the volcanoes. Where are you from?"

"Near Chicago, but I was in Cameroon before this."

"For the Peace Corps also?

"Yes. . . . I had problems in my village, and they found me a place here, to do youth development work instead of health education. It fits my background better, anyway. Where are you from?"

"San Francisco area. I've been here almost two years, and I'll be finished with my service soon. I work with runaways and at-risk kids. We do challenge education activities. It's very fulfilling."

Jessie noticed that the people around them were all slapping their legs and arms, trying to kill mosquitoes. She remembered a moment with Daniel in France when she'd experienced the same thing. Then she noticed that there were no mosquitoes near them.

"I'm really looking forward to working with children too," she said. "Hey, did you notice that everyone around us is getting attacked by mosquitoes?"

Christopher looked around. "You're right, but I'm not getting bitten. Are you?"

"No, that's what's strange."

"Are you following your heart?" he asked.

Jessie gave him a strange look, but didn't reply.

Christopher smiled knowingly. "If you're following your

heart, then you've probably changed the electromagnetic field around you. Everybody has one."

"Are you saying that the mosquitoes are leaving me alone because of some electromagnetic field?" she said, laughing.

Christopher looked embarrassed. "Well, no. I wasn't saying that. It was sort of a joke, but not entirely." He smiled sheepishly.

"If you wanted to tell me that my energy feels different, then I would understand better," Jessie said, returning the smile.

"Yes, that's what I wanted to tell you."

They both chuckled.

"So what's your long-term goal? Do you plan to keep working in youth education?" asked Jessie.

"I want to go back to school and get a doctorate in theosophy. Then I'd like to become a professor, conduct research, and teach."

If the Word sent Christopher here to help me, Jessie thought, then he should know something about love. "Please don't take this the wrong way," she said, "but since you are religious and philosophical, you've probably studied love, right?"

Christopher chewed his food, nodding.

"So why do you think we fall in love with one person rather than another? Or the person we choose to love falls in love with someone else?"

Christopher chuckled. "From my studies, and my own personal experience, I think attraction is often confused with love," he said. "Attraction is what draws us to another person. Basically that person has something that we think we want."

"Go on . . ."

"When our mind discovers that the same person also has something that we *don't* want, the relationship changes. Now it's based on something bigger: truth."

Jessie opened her mouth, but Christopher held up one finger to communicate that he would like to finish.

"Love happens after attraction, and after the truth has been revealed. A delicate balance takes form with two free individuals connecting from the heart. They begin to feed each other, instead of feeding themselves with the other. And the real magic begins."

"So it's the truth that allows them to become more in touch with themselves and their purpose in this world."

"Yes, with attraction and balance in place. In a nonromantic way, it's like Jesus. It was the truth of humankind, in all its beauty and ugliness that led him to give himself for their salvation."

"You are incredibly intelligent," said Jessie.

Christopher looked down bashfully. "What are you doing after training today?" he asked.

"I need to start running again."

"Running is bad on your knees," he said. "Would you be interested in walking with me a few times a week? I would love to talk more."

"Sure, okay, that would be great."

"It's nice to be around someone who understands me."

Jessie smiled sweetly.

They finished their lunch, and Jessie went back to class. She felt freer, dwelling on the conversation she had with Christopher, and loving Daniel more.

On their next rendezvous, Christopher took Jessie to his favorite suburb: Guapulo. Situated on a small plateau in the hills between Quito and the Tumbaco Valley, on the road taken by Francisco

Pizarro's expedition, it had been a place of pilgrimage for many centuries.

They entered a church, a mix of neoclassic and Baroque design from the sixteenth century with massive twisted Moorish columns, and adorned with paintings and sculptures by Indian artists. A statue of the Virgin of Guadalupe stood in the niche behind the pulpit, set into a magnificent gilded reredos.

Christopher approached the altar, kneeled beside it, and put his forehead on the floor, staying there for a long time as he prayed. Jessie remembered Iya praying in a similar way. When he was done, they sat down on a pew in front.

"I didn't know you were Catholic," said Jessie.

"I was raised this way. It's kind of in my blood, but I don't subscribe to the doctrine of the church."

"Who was the Virgin of Guadalupe, anyway?"

"She's an icon of the Virgin Mary. Juan Diego, the first indigenous saint, saw a vision of a girl of fifteen or sixteen years of age, surrounded by light. The girl told him to build a church in her honor."

"And why were you praying to an icon?"

"I wasn't praying *to* her, or to anyone else. I was having a conversation with God."

"A conversation with God?"

"I was saying the Lord's Prayer."

Jessie gave him a strange look. "You don't appear to be the type who heaps up empty phrases to God."

Christopher looked shocked. "Empty phrases? No way! I meant every word."

"When I pray, nothing happens. I don't know why."

"Probably because you're not praying the right way. If you're just asking for things for you, then forget it."

"So how do *you* pray?"

"I know what I'm asking, and that God will answer. 'Your kingdom come, your will be done, on earth as it is in heaven.' You have to taste it, smell it, see it, hear it in your mind and feel it in your heart, before you can expect it to happen. Prayer comes from the source of creation, deep feeling from the core of your being. Words happen, things begin, inside the heart."

Jessie was nodding, once again amazed by his intelligence. I never prayed for Daniel, she thought. I was always praying for myself.

That night, before going to sleep, Jessie wrote in her journal and then prayed for Daniel. She envisioned him happy, in a place full of truth and love, having found the answer he'd searched so tirelessly for. Finally he had found his spiritual elixir, eternal life in harmony with the divine.

A few weeks later, when Christopher and Jessie were walking, they came across a narrow dirt road. Curious, they decided to follow it. They walked over a hill and through a stretch of forest, then came to a clearing that held what looked like a huge community garden. In one section, baskets full of carrots had been left on the ground. Christopher reached down and picked a carrot up. "Look at the size of these. It's the rich volcanic soil that makes them so large."

"I love gardens," said Jessie.

"Me, too!"

They continued walking, past the peppers to the green beans. Jessie bent down to pick one, but they were full of wormholes. "If it weren't for all the invasion, gardens would be a paradise," she said. "Eden was supposed to be a paradise."

"Supposed to be? Do you mean to say it wasn't?"

"How could it be, with the tree of the knowledge of good and evil? There was evil in the garden!"

"I know the story, but what's your point?"

"It was God's garden," said Jessie. "Why was there knowledge of evil in God's precious garden? Why was there knowledge of evil in God? Everything in the garden and in God should have been good, unless—"

"Unless what? Who knows why God had knowledge of evil, but I know without a shadow of doubt that God is good."

"I want to believe in the goodness of God, but I don't understand him or that tree. Instead of taking it away, he told Adam and Eve not to eat of it."

"They didn't obey God, and that was the problem, but what you see is the tree. You want to know why it was there in the first place," said Christopher. "Is that right?"

"Yes, that tree is a source of conflict for me. I think about all the reasons why it could have been there, twisting my brain into knots. Was the tree a symbol of God's own good and evil? Did he really expect Adam and Eve to ignore this hot-pink elephant in the garden?"

Christopher was quiet, listening carefully, while Jessie continued to argue with herself. "Sure enough, Adam and Eve fell into temptation, but what happened next isn't consistent with my understanding of love. He sent Adam and Eve away and left the tree in the garden. He left the source of evil."

"And he left the source of good! The tree of knowledge was both good and evil. Obviously they're inseparable."

Jessie fell into deep thought, desperately searching for an explanation. "So there are only two possibilities," she said finally. "God is half evil—and I can't believe this—or God created something good that turned evil, Lucifer became Satan. If I follow the Lucifer-Satan story, then I have to ask myself why God didn't destroy Satan, why he exiled us from the garden but let Satan stay, and why he lets Satan pursue us even now."

"And you said that I think too much?" Christopher exclaimed. "Jessie, God is love! He loved Lucifer, and he still does. What if you had a child and you loved that child, but he chose not to love you and not to love in general. Your child went even further, hurting everything and everyone he touched. Would you destroy your child? No, you'd love your child! You'd be hoping that something, somewhere, somehow, would bring him home."

Jessie sighed, still thinking. "Are you saying that the reason for the tree and for the knowledge of evil is that God couldn't and wouldn't part from his child who was carrying it?"

"Yes!"

"But then why did he create us? He knew Satan was here! He knew Satan would go after us and try to destroy us! Still, he threw us into a mess and created a maze that we'd have to wriggle our way through. That's not a loving thing to do."

Christopher nodded, thinking, as they continued walking through the garden. The tomato plants were sick, too; the leaves were spotted with black, and the fruit were full of holes.

"I don't know all the answers, but I will remind you to follow your heart. We aren't capable of understanding everything with our minds. There are too many contradictions and too many holes, even in our own behavior. We know this world is big and bad, but we still have children. We know they will go through tough times, and other people may try to hurt them, but we love our children through it all."

Christopher found a tomato without any wormholes and handed it to Jessie with a big smile. It looked like he was trying to tell her something without words.

"You're right, Christopher. I understand."

He chuckled and put his arm around Jessie.

"If I had to guess what happened up there, I would say something went very wrong. But through us, God has a plan to fix it all with his nature. Love is the nature of God, and Jesus Christ showed us what it was all about."

"Of course," said Jessie.

In that moment, she knew without a shadow of doubt that Christopher was sent by the Word. He was too wise in the ways that she needed; it couldn't just be a coincidence.

"It is said we were made to co-create," said Jessie, "but collaboration makes more sense in the grand scheme of things. If we can really love, it can change everything."

Christopher nodded. "It's time for a new garden."

Jessie wiped off her tomato and took a bite. It was juicy and sweet.

"Yes, a new garden would be nice, one with pure love and no evil. That's where I've always imagined God and eternal life to be."

"So create one," said Christopher, grinning. "You know how—you're clever."

Jessie stood up straight and smiled. "Maybe I will."

15
The Garden

Three months passed and training was over. Jessie had been assigned to an orphanage run by a private organization in the southwest city of Machala. Teary eyed, she said good-bye to her good friend Christopher, who was going back to San Francisco. Then she traveled to her new post, and moved into a small apartment by herself.

Her workplace was a neglected stucco house with big cracks in the walls. The yard was strewn with trash, and weeds struggled up from the dusty ground. She opened the door halfway and peered inside. A gray mouse scurried through the passage, squeaking.

"Hello . . . is anybody here?" she asked, stepping in nervously. The house smelled awful. The place was filthy. Several bags of trash were piled up in the corner, next to a dirty litter box. A cat was sleeping on the couch.

Jessie sneezed, and an angry-looking man in black pants and a shabby T-shirt appeared from around the corner. His hair was oily and stringy, and his hands were covered in dirt.

"Can I help you?" he asked grumpily.

"Hi. I'm Jessie, the new Peace Corps volunteer."

Jessie extended her arm to shake the man's hand, but he just turned around and started walking away. Jessie stood there, not sure what to do. "Follow me," he said, several steps ahead.

Jessie followed him to a door, which was closed. He pointed at it apathetically and walked away.

"Thank you very much," said Jessie as he disappeared behind the corner. Taking a deep breath, she knocked on the door.

"What do you want?" someone yelled inside.

Without responding, Jessie pushed open the door. A woman with black hair pulled back in a ponytail jumped up from her chair. She appeared to be watching television.

"Can I help you?" she asked irritably. Jessie wondered if she was disturbing her, or whether it was a bad time.

"Hi, I'm Jessie, your new Peace Corps volunteer."

The woman forced a smile and shook Jessie's hand. Then she sat back down at her desk. There were no pictures on the wall, and no other chairs. Her desk was empty except for a coffee cup. She was watching a soap opera.

"Well, thank you for coming. The children are outside. Go around the corner and walk all the way down the hall to the back door."

That's all she has to say? Jessie thought. She looks so angry.

She smiled politely, quietly closing the door as she left. In the back, children were running around a large fenced yard that looked like an enclosure in a zoo.

A baby's cry rose above the screeching voices, and Jessie followed it to an addition behind the house. She walked into a room full of babies. Carefully she picked up the one who'd been crying so loudly, looking into his big brown eyes. He stopped crying and smiled at Jessie.

"I think his diaper needs changing," said a girl nearby.

Two other girls walked over to see what was going on.

"Who are you?" asked one of them.

"I'm Jessie . . . and you?"

"I'm Martha."

"I'm Ruth."

"And I'm Clara."

"It's very nice to meet you. Do you know where I can find a diaper?" asked Jessie.

"They're all gone, but there are some towels in the bathroom," replied one of the girls.

They led Jessie to the nearest bathroom. When they walked in, a toddler was drinking from the toilet.

"Don't do that!" said Jessie. "We don't drink out of the toilet unless we want to get very sick."

Martha stepped between Jessie and the child. "It's just because we're not allowed to eat and drink between meals."

"Sinks are better than toilets," replied Jessie.

"But he can't reach," said Martha, speaking again for the child. "And there's nothing to stand on."

"Then lift him," responded Jessie.

Martha lifted the child to the sink while Jessie found a dingy towel in the cabinet. She smelled it but couldn't tell if it was clean. With no other alternative, she rinsed the baby off and wrapped him in the towel.

When she went back outside, she found another young boy in trouble, sucking from a methane tank. Shocked, she wondered what was going on in this place. "Ruth, I need your help."

Ruth removed the boy from the tank, and Jessie returned the baby to his crib. On the way back, a little girl walked by with scissors in her hand and a large patch of missing hair. Jessie sat the girl down and looked her in the eyes.

"We don't walk around with scissors pointing up like this," she said sternly. "You or someone else could get hurt, my little sweetheart."

At the end of the day, Jessie was exhausted. She went home, fell backward into bed, put a pillow over her face, and lay there. She stayed awake only a few minutes. No food, no writing, just sleep.

The next day she went to find the director. Afraid to knock, she pressed her ear against the door and listened; someone was coming. As she stepped around the corner, the director walked out in the hallway and lit up a cigarette. Then she glanced through the messages on her cell phone. Jessie waited for her to take a puff of smoke before she rounded the corner again, taking her by surprise.

"Sorry, I forgot to ask your name yesterday," she said.

"Elda," the woman replied tersely.

"Ms. Elda, how can we get some more supplies like diapers, soap, and paper towels?"

Elda's lips tightened. She led Jessie to a storage room in another part of the house.

"Here's where we keep the stuff. The Peace Corps will help if you need more."

The room smelled awful, and the shelves were covered with dust and mouse droppings. As Jessie shuffled around, a bag of rotten potatoes fell to the floor. After a thorough search, she had found nothing they could use. She took the potatoes to the trash, discouraged. It didn't seem as if Elda cared about her job, or the children either.

Frustrated, Jessie went out back and pulled together the three girls who'd helped her the day before. They looked nervous. "Thank you for your help yesterday," she said warmly. "Is something wrong?"

The girls lowered their eyes.

"Come on, what's going on?"

"You're not going to leave us, are you?"

"No! Why would you think that?"

"Because everybody leaves us."

Trying not to cry, Jessie made a funny face. "It's not *you*, silly girls . . . it's the smell. They just can't stand that awful smell!"

Martha and Ruth looked at each other and started laughing. Clara clenched her fists nervously. Jessie had only one goal: to fix the problem.

"Don't worry, we're going to change the smell of this place. We have to catch the right smells first," she said, thinking fondly of her time with Daniel by the sea.

Clara rolled her eyes. "Are you joking?" she said condescendingly.

Without answering, Jessie organized a game. She asked all the children to go catch the smells that they liked and bring them back to the group to share. One girl came back smiling, with a flower in her hand.

"Ahhhh, this flower has a nice smell," Jessie said. "You brought the flower, but did you catch the smell?" "You can't catch smells," said the girl, giggling.

Jessie smiled. "Are you sure?"

Soon all the children had gathered in a circle, each carrying something. Jessie asked them to explain what they'd brought. Several girls had flowers, one boy had a bar of soap, and another had a piece of candy.

"Hey, where'd you get candy?" said one of the boys.

"Ms. Jessie, he's not sharing!" said another.

"I want some, too!" said yet another.

Jessie walked over to Martha, who was holding a baby. Then she closed her eyes and smelled the baby's head.

"Okay, you found things that had smells you liked, but you didn't catch the actual smells! Come . . . smell the baby's head," said Jessie, "and see what I mean."

Laughing, the children lined up and took turns.

"Now what did you catch? I caught a glimpse of heaven. I can feel it now, and it's wonderful!"

There was a healthy silence.

"Peace," said Martha.

"Good!" replied Jessie.

"Innocence," said another child.

"Love."

"Happiness."

"Good. Good! Now pretend that everyone is a smell and run around and catch each other."

The children skedaddled everywhere, running around each other as fast as they could, laughing. Jessie giggled, seeing them so happy.

Six o'clock passed, and Jessie was still there. She stayed late, helping the children get ready for bed and reading them stories. Then she spent some time cleaning. It was around midnight before she called a taxi to take her home. While waiting for it to come, she silently thanked Daniel for giving her the idea about smells.

In this moment, Daniel is under the sun, she thought, and I am under the moon.

When she got home, she took a few deep breaths and fell

asleep. She dreamed of a big garden—a new garden, like Eden. It was a place filled with tremendous love, both intelligence and feeling, but without a trace of evil. There was no sadness or pain, just peace, joy, and hope for the dreams of divine.

Jessie woke up early for a morning run. On her way home she bought all kinds of seeds, twenty small shovels, and several hoes. Luckily her apartment was right around the corner, and some boys helped her carry the stuff up. After showering, she put it all in a big bag and called a taxi to go to work.

As soon as the children saw her, they came running.

"Look, it's a bag of toys!"

"I told you Jessie knew Santa Claus."

"Ms. Jessie, what did you bring?"

She put the bag down, and the children peeked inside. They looked confused.

"We're going to make a garden!" said Jessie.

"What?" said a boy. "But that's work!"

"Yes, but it will be fun. It's not an ordinary garden; it's a magic garden, and I know how to do it."

"Really?" said a girl, jumping up and down.

"Okay! What kind of magic?"

"It's a garden where we can create anything we want. We can grow delicious foods, fabulous smells, good feelings, music, colors you've never imagined, green cows with purple ears . . . a place where dreams come true."

The children laughed.

"Let's do it," said Ruth. "In the back, away from the house and the smell, is a good place to grow things."

The older children used the hoes to clear away the weeds. It took them all morning. In the afternoon, after lunch, the younger children made the holes. Jessie helped them along until it was time to plant the seeds.

"Okay, everyone, close your eyes and imagine what you want

to grow in this garden and in your life. Think only happy, loving, peaceful things."

While their eyes were closed, Jessie went around and put some seeds in the hands of each child.

"Now open your eyes and plant whatever it is that your heart desires," she said. "Put it in the ground."

After they'd planted all their seeds, Jessie had them hold hands around the garden.

"We are going to pray now," she said. "Do not ask for what you planted; give it your heart, catch the feeling you will have when it grows up, and thank God for it."

The children looked confused. Jessie thought about what she'd learned, about how there is no future tense in Fulfulde or Hebrew, about how everything in those languages exists in the here and now. How could she help the children understand?

"Okay, when I say go, you're going to jump, sing, smile, and laugh, because God has already answered your prayer. There's no *future* for your prayer. It's right here and now. You already have it. On your mark, get set, go!"

All the children started laughing, screaming, jumping up and down. They did this for several minutes before they went inside to have dinner, excited and happy. Jessie went home exhausted once again, and fell into bed. Her body was relaxed and ready for sleep, but she really wanted to write. She took several deep breaths and opened her journal.

I feel the love growing . . .

The pen fell from her hand, and she was asleep.

The next morning, when Jessie arrived, a little girl was screaming. When she went to see what was happening, she found Elda beating the girl with a stick.

"What are you doing?"

As soon as Elda saw Jessie, she straightened. "She pooped her pants again."

"Don't worry, I'll take care of her." Jessie walked the little girl to the bathroom and cleaned her up. When she came back, Elda had disappeared. Jessie called the Peace Corps in Quito, in tears, begging for them to do something. Her superiors immediately informed the authorities in Machala. It took a couple hours, but an officer from the Ministry of Social Welfare was sent to investigate.

After talking with Jessie and looking around carefully, the officer moved to shut down the orphanage and relocate the children. Everyone was flabbergasted. Workers had come and gone for years, and complaints had never been addressed before. Elda was still nowhere to be found.

While the officer made phone calls, Jessie went out back to calm down the children.

"Ms. Jessie, yesterday when we were making the garden, many of us prayed for this to happen. It really works!" said Martha.

"Now they are going to put us in a nicer place," said Clara, with a big smile.

Jessie realized that all of them, including her, had planted the same seed. She smiled back and nodded, hoping she'd done the right thing. It felt right in her heart, but she was also a little nervous, and didn't know why.

The officer came out to ask for help, and Jessie went in. Carefully they lined the children up and loaded them into vehicles, and Jessie escorted them to the new location. There were many child-care workers at the facility; it looked clean and caring.

"Ms. Jessie, it smells good here," said a child. Jessie nodded, laughed, and hugged her. This time, she didn't hold back her tears.

When Jessie returned home, it was late again. Exhausted, she ate a light dinner and crawled into bed with her journal. Soon afterward, the phone rang. It was Daniel.

"Hi, Jessie, I got all your letters. Listen, I don't want to fight with you anymore. We need to talk. . . . I'm coming this weekend."

Jessie was shocked; it had been such a long time since he'd spoken to her, and now he was coming to visit? Was it about their research or his feelings?

"Wow! You're coming all the way to Ecuador? That's great news. I have a spare bedroom, if you want."

There was a moment of silence. "A spare bedroom? Okay, it doesn't matter. Listen, I found the meaning of the symbols."

"Really?"

"They're Adamic . . . the language that was spoken by Adam and Eve in the Garden of Eden."

"I've never heard of this language."

"It's not clear whether it started with God, addressing Adam, or with Adam, when he named all things, but it's the beginning of human language."

"Well, what do the symbols mean?"

Daniel took a deep breath. "After a lot of investigation, I found that together they form a word that means 'bridges.' "

Jessie was quiet, thinking.

"Don't you see?" said Daniel. "The book builds bridges to the place we came from."

"Of course!" said Jessie. "It describes perfectly the intelligence of love. Love bridges all barriers back to the Word, through harmony, to fulfill a master plan."

"Mmm . . . I think you're missing the point. This book came from the Garden of Eden, the beginning of language and humankind. It shows the way back in time—the way to start over."

"Start over? In the Garden of Eden?"

"I know it sounds crazy. We'll talk more when I see you. I need to explain in person."

"Is everything okay?" asked Jessie. "You sound a little strange, or troubled."

"When I discovered the purpose of the book, I had a realization about myself," Daniel whispered.

"What about?"

"I can't tell you on the phone, but honestly, I don't deserve your love. I love you, but I don't deserve you."

"That's so sweet, but love is not something we can deserve," Jessie said. "I love you, too, but I don't deserve you either. I make so many mistakes."

"You don't know who I really am, or all the things I have done. I am bad—nobody could love the real me."

Jessie sensed that he was sorry and sad.

"I don't know what you want to tell me, Daniel, but nothing can change the fact that my heart is exploding with love for you. It's not a fantasy like before; it's an intelligence that I am obliged to follow."

"Come on, Jessie. Even the divine has rejected me, without any means for salvation."

"Those are really strong words, Daniel. What exactly do you mean?"

"I can't tell you more until I see you this weekend. I'm sorry, Jessie. I have to go now."

Jessie was concerned for Daniel. It was strange that he was coming all the way to Ecuador just to tell her something. He didn't sound well.

After tossing and turning most of the night, she woke from

a nightmare in the early morning hours. Nervous and tense, she found her journal and wrote it down.

I was sitting in the sand beside the sea with the ancient book on my lap, listening to the wind and waves perform. The book was composing, and I was preparing myself to conduct the next performance. When the sun started to set, the boy came in with the tide, and my heart swelled with love. He put his hands and feet on the book. Was he trying to stop it from composing? Or was he trying to get inside? When I asked, he turned, and I saw his face for the first time. It was the face of Daniel. His eyes were red and crazed, and he was grinning. "I am bad," he said. "Do not love me."

There was a noise, and Jessie jumped up. Sensing an intruder, she looked around the house, but nobody was there. The sun was rising, and she felt unsettled. She needed to calm down, so she slipped on her running shoes and headed out the door.

The hallway was dark; she could barely see the stairs. Using her hands to feel the wall, she stepped carefully. Once outside, she began jogging down the road, deep in thought.

She recalled the tarantula's omen, and what had happened next. The ancient book had come into her life, setting off a series of strange occurrences. She'd been cast into darkness, and Daniel became her light. Later, he'd thrown her into darkness, but she could not let him go. It was as if he had become a deep part of her.

Who is this Daniel, and what is this bond we share? He is both my help and hindrance, the subject and object of my love.

Back at the house, she started trotting up the stairs to her apartment. About halfway up she stopped, exhausted, to catch her breath. She walked the rest of the way, breathing heavily.

Dimly she saw the figure of a woman standing at the top of the stairs. As she drew closer, she could see that it was Elda.

She swallowed a lump in her throat. What was Elda doing here? She didn't have a good feeling about this. A few steps away, she could see that Elda was glaring at her viciously. She wanted to turn around, but it was too late.

"Elda, you disappeared, and I never had a chance to say good-bye—"

"Why did you have to interfere?" Elda's voice vibrated with fury. "My father left me when I was a girl. My stepfather abused me physically, and then my husband."

Elda pointed to her black eye, and Jessie nodded, her internal alarm going haywire.

Elda had had a hard life, like me. I wasn't thinking about her. I didn't pray for her. I just wanted to help the children. Is she going to kill me now? Am I going to die?

"When I told my husband that I'd lost my job, he beat me and threw me out of the house. I have no money, and nowhere to go."

Jessie's eyes filled with tears; she was afraid for her life, and sorry that she hadn't thought of a way to help both the children and Elda. Unable to think of anything to say, she nodded to show that she was listening, and took a step forward. She wanted to hug Elda. She wanted to be there now.

"And you know the worst of it?" said Elda. "Nobody gives a damn! Nobody cares!"

The words pierced Jessie's heart, and the realization struck her like a blow: *Everyone is hurting in some way. This is why they hurt other people.* At that moment she instinctively knew the only way to break the cycle. The words fell into her heart.

Forgive and love the people who hurt you.

"I'm so sorry, Elda. I care. Let me help you, please," she said with a sob, still stepping forward.

Elda lunged toward her. Pushed off balance, she tumbled backward, and everything went black.

I forgive my father for leaving me. I forgive my sensei for taking advantage of me. I forgive Daniel for hurting me deeply. I forgive Elda for abusing the children. And I forgive myself for not seeing other people's pain, and for not praying for Elda. Elda's anger comes from deep hurt, and she needs love.

Soft music surrounded her like the breath of the divine, unlike anything she had ever heard. Extraordinary smells filled the air. They were everywhere, breathing and moving in the garden.

A ball of magnificent colors landed on Jessie's hand. Her body pulsed with tenderness and affection, and the ball exploded into a living bird, its throat stretched in celestial song as it flew around her.

"Do you like this place?"

Jessie looked beside her.

"Daniel! What are you doing here?"

"You brought me here."

"I did? Where are we?"

"I don't know. The last thing I recall is that someone had broken into my house. He couldn't find the ancient book, and he was threatening me. Suddenly you were carrying me. Then I was carrying you. Now we are here."

"How strange—now I remember. We were flying, and then we landed in something fluffy and soft."

He pointed to the horizon: a gigantic mountain that looked like cotton.

"I thought it was a dream." She touched his shoulder, and her whole body tingled. "I've never felt so much from a touch."

"I've never felt so free," said Daniel. "It's amazing. Look! I have wings."

He flew up and around to show Jessie, and she laughed. It was all becoming clear. "I know this place. This is the garden I dreamed about. Think of something you wish to create."

Before them appeared a row of trees with a variety of rich colors and fragrances. On one, the fruit looked like little suns; on another, like moons; on yet another, stars. All the fruit was singing.

"Wow!" said Daniel. "It's exactly as I imagined."

"Now try to create something evil."

Daniel tried, but he couldn't. His mind would not move in that direction. Jessie watched him struggle and laughed affectionately.

"In this garden," she said, "there is no tree of the knowledge of good and evil, as there was in the Garden of Eden. There is no serpent or Satan either. It's a garden of pure love."

"You made this?" asked Daniel, puzzled.

"Well, I imagined it, I prayed it, but I can't say that I made it."

"If you imagined it and you prayed it, you had to have made it somehow. Otherwise it wouldn't exist."

"Perhaps the Word made it through me. All I did was try to follow my heart. We cannot possess love or anything here; we can only be possessed by it."

Something stroked Jessie's hair.

"Wake up!" thundered a voice.

"What was that?"

"You have to go," Daniel said. "I saved you."

"From what?"

"From that woman, and the fall."

She was floating up from the garden.

"What were you going to tell me?"

"I don't remember," he called out. "But I'll be right here, waiting for you to return."

"Open your eyes!" said the voice again.

She was lying in a bed. An unfamiliar face was staring down at her. She felt heavy, and her head was pounding.

"She's awake!" said the man standing over her. "I'm Dr. Eduardo. You fell down the stairs."

"The last thing I remember is Elda. She pushed me, I think . . ."

"You were found at the bottom of a stairwell. If someone pushed you, then you'll need to tell the police. You have a concussion, and you were in a coma for three days."

The doctor left, and the nurse came in with her chart.

"Okay, how many fingers am I holding up?"

"Four."

"I want you to slowly repeat what I say after ten seconds . . . seven elephants jumped over a fence."

Jessie repeated the phrase.

"Well, your brain is working properly. That's pretty amazing, considering what you've been through."

Jessie nodded, relieved.

"We haven't been able to reach your emergency contact. According to your Peace Corps paperwork, it's Daniel Lumiel, correct?"

"You didn't try my mother or brother?" asked Jessie.

The nurse looked over her paperwork again.

"No. They are not listed here. Would you like us to contact them?"

"That's very strange. I thought they had my paperwork from before. I thought I was just adding Daniel."

"Is Mr. Lumiel your father?"

"Oh, no, he's a good friend."

"This may sound strange, but I was just reading the story about Lumiel," said the nurse.

"What do you mean?"

"Lumiel is a fallen angel. He fell because he disobeyed the Creator, trying to speed up mankind's evolution. He wanted to give people knowledge before they had the wisdom to use it correctly."

Jessie sat up, flabbergasted.

"Lucifer is the only fallen angel I've heard about."

"Oh, no, there are many."

"Where do they all go?"

"Some go to work as demons. Others live like humans in the world, trying to get back to where they came from. There's no plan of salvation for fallen angels, so they have no other options."

Jessie bit her lip. This is what made the world a mess, she thought.

"Anyway," the nurse said, seeing that Jessie was nervous, "several people came to visit you and prayed for you. They will be very happy to see you."

Jessie touched the bandage on her head. "Can I have a mirror, please?"

The nurse hesitated, but eventually brought one. Jessie was horrified. Her hair was shaved all around the bandage, and the whole side of her face was black and blue. A few tears dripped down her cheeks.

"Don't worry," said the nurse. "It's not bad . . . it will heal. Just be thankful you're alive. There's some angel watching over you, that's for sure. Seriously, honey, such an accident would have killed most people."

Did Daniel really save me? Did I save him first?

The nurse smiled and handed Jessie a box that held many drawings from the children, and her mail from the Peace Corps office. There was also a package with no return address. Jessie opened it carefully, and stared, amazed.

"What's that?" asked the nurse.

"It's an ancient book. It belongs to Daniel. Excuse me, but is there a way that I can call him?"

"Sure, let me take you to the phone."

Jessie tried the number many times, but no one answered. She opened the book and gazed at a page. Suddenly she became aware of the same soft music she'd heard in her dream. She looked around to see where it was coming from, but she could not find a source. It was everywhere.

"Excuse me," she said to the nurse, who was writing notes in her file. "Do you hear music?"

The nurse stopped what she was doing and listened.

"Oh, yes . . . it's lovely. I've never heard it before."

Jessie looked back into the book. Waves of colors and smells floated out of it. The new garden from her dream took form, startling her. She couldn't believe her eyes, so she closed them for a moment. When she pulled back and looked into her own reflection on the page, the face staring back at her was Daniel's.

Her heart poured out, filling her body with divine love. A transmutation was taking place, harmonic and eternal.

There is Daniel, in the garden that I conceived, with wings. How can this be?

Back at her apartment, she opened her journal, desperately seeking an answer. A new line had appeared.

The miracle is in your heart.

Author Bio

Wendy Sue Williamson is a veteran study-abroad director and
Returned Peace Corps Volunteer (RPCV), with a background
in communication and culture. A graduate of Indiana University and Western Michigan University, she is the author of
Study Abroad 101, a best seller in student travel guides. Wendy
lives in Italy with her family. In addition to writing, she enjoys
traveling, spending time with loved ones, meeting new people,
exploring the great outdoors, balanced living, and slow food.

Follow the Author

wswilliamson.com
facebook.com/wswilliamson
twitter.com/wswilliamson
linkedin.com/in/wswilliamson

Follow the Publisher

agapy.com
facebook.com/agapyllc

CPSIA information can be obtained at www.ICGtesting.com
Printed in the USA
LVOW01s1815140714

394272LV00036B/2148/P